When I'm Gone

ALSO BY ABBI GLINES

In publication order by series

The Rosemary Beach Series
Fallen Too Far
Never Too Far
Forever Too Far
Twisted Perfection
Simple Perfection
Take a Chance
Rush Too Far
One More Chance
You Were Mine
Kiro's Emily (novella)

The Sea Breeze Series
Breathe
Because of Low
While It Lasts
Just for Now
Sometimes It Lasts
Misbehaving
Bad for You
Hold on Tight
Until the End

The Vincent Boys Series
The Vincent Boys
The Vincent Brothers

The Existence Series
Existence
Predestined
Ceaseless

When I'm Gone

Gone

A Rosemary Beach Novel

Abbi Glines

ATRIA PAPERBACK

New York • London • Toronto • Sydney • New Delhi

ATRIA PAPERBACK

A Division of Simon & Schuster, Inc.

1230 Avenue of the Americas

New York, NY 10020

First Atria Paperback edition April 2015

ATRIA PAPERBACK and colophon are trademarks of Simon & Schuster, Inc.

For information about special discounts for bulk purchases, please contact Simon & Schuster Special Sales at 1-866-506-1949 or business@simonandschuster.com.

The Simon & Schuster Speakers Bureau can bring authors to your live event. For more information or to book an event, contact the Simon & Schuster Speakers Bureau at 1-866-248-3049 or visit our website at www.simonspeakers.com.

Interior design by Dana Sloan

Manufactured in the United States of America

10 9 8 7 6 5 4 3 2 1

Library of Congress Cataloging-in-Publication Data is available.

ISBN 978-1-4767-7609-5
ISBN 978-1-4767-7610-1 (ebook)

*To my son, Austin. May you become a man
who is thoughtful, kind, considerate, giving, and
knows how to really love someone. Those men
are hard to find. I hope I'm raising one.*

Prologue

Reese

"Come here, girl!" My stepfather's voice bellowed throughout the house.

Instantly, my gut twisted. The sick knot that came from being near him and knowing what he would do to me was a constant companion.

I stood up slowly from my bed and put the book I was reading—or trying to read—down carefully. My mother wasn't home from work yet. She was supposed to be home by now. I shouldn't have come back from the library so early. A man and his young daughter had come up to me while I was looking through the children's picture books. He'd started talking to me and asking me my name. He'd wanted to know if I was getting a book for my little sister.

The embarrassment that came with that question reminded me of my stupidity, as always.

"Girl!" my stepfather roared.

He was angry now. My eyes stung with unshed tears. If he would only just beat me like he used to. Back when I was younger and I brought home poor grades in school. If he

1

would just call me names and tell me how worthless I was . . . but he wouldn't. Once I had wished more than anything that he would stop hitting me. I hated the belt, and the welts he left on my legs and bottom made it hard to sit down.

Then one day, he stopped. And I instantly wished he'd go back to hitting me. The bite from the belt was better than this. Anything was better than this. Even death.

I opened my bedroom door and took a deep breath, reminding myself that I could survive whatever he did. I was saving my money from the housecleaning jobs I had, and I would be leaving here soon. My mother would be glad I was gone. She hated me. She had hated me for years.

I was a burden on her.

I tugged my shirt down and tucked it into the shorts I was wearing. Then I pulled the shorts down so they covered more of my legs. It was pointless, really. I had long legs that were hard to cover up. There were never any shorts at the thrift store long enough.

It was only an hour before my mother got home. He wouldn't do anything that she could walk in on. Even if she did, I wondered if she would accuse me and say it was my fault. She had already blamed me for the way my body had changed four years ago. My breasts had grown too large, and she said I needed to stop eating because my ass was fat. I had tried not eating, but it hadn't helped my bottom.

My stomach had flattened out, and it had only made my chest look larger. She hated that. So I started eating again, but my stomach pudge never returned. One night, when I had walked into the living room in a pair of cutoff sweatpants and a T-shirt to get some milk before I went to bed, she slapped me and told me I looked like a whore. More than once, she called me a stupid whore who had nothing but her looks to get her anywhere in life.

Now I stepped into the living room to see Marco, my step-father, sitting in his recliner with his eyes trained on the television and a beer in his hand. He had come home from work early.

His gaze swung to me and slowly trailed up my body, making me shiver with disgust. What I wouldn't give to be smart and flat-chested. If my legs were short and fat, then my life would be perfect. My face wasn't what attracted Marco. It was average enough. I hated my body. I hated it so much.

Nausea crept up, and my heart raced as I fought back the tears. He loved it when I cried. It made him worse. I wouldn't cry. Not in front of him.

"Come sit in my lap," he ordered.

I couldn't do it. I had been able to avoid him for weeks by staying away from the house as much as possible. The horror of having his hands up my shirt or in my pants again was too much. I'd rather he killed me. Anything but this.

When I didn't move, his face twisted into an evil sneer. "Get your stupid slutty ass over here, and sit on my goddamn lap!"

I closed my eyes, because the tears were coming. I had to stop them. If he'd just hit me again, I'd take it. I just couldn't stand him touching me. I hated the sounds he made and the things he said. It was a never-ending nightmare.

Every second I stayed back was a second closer to my mother getting home. When she was here, he called me names, but he never touched me. She might wish I didn't exist, but she was my only salvation from this.

"Go ahead and cry, I like it," he said, sneering.

His chair creaked, and then I heard the footrest slam down. I snapped my eyes open to see him standing up. Not good. If I ran, I wouldn't make it past him. The only other option was the backyard, but his pit bull was out there. It had bitten me three years ago, and I had needed stitches, but he hadn't let me go to the doctor. He'd told me to wrap it up; he wasn't putting his dog down over my stupid ass.

I had an ugly scar on my hip from the dog's teeth.

I'd never gone into the backyard again.

But watching him walk toward me, I wondered if being eaten by his dog wasn't better than this. It was a means to an end: death. Which didn't sound so bad.

Just before he reached me, I decided that whatever his dog would do to me was better than this. So I ran.

He cackled with laughter behind me, but I didn't let it slow me down. He didn't think I'd go out the back door. How wrong he was. I would face the dogs of hell to get away from him.

But the door was bolted. I needed the key to unbolt it. *No. No.*

His hands grabbed my waist and pulled me back to feel his hardness pressing against me. The sour taste of vomit burned the back of my throat as I jerked away from him. "No!" I yelled.

His hands moved around and grabbed my breasts and squeezed painfully. "Stupid whore. This is all you're good for. Couldn't graduate from high school because you were too damn stupid. But this body is meant to make men happy. Accept that, bitch."

The tears ran down my face. I hadn't been able to stop them. He knew the words to hurt me. "No!" I cried out again, but this time the pain was there in my voice. It cracked.

"Fight me, Reese. I like it when you fight me," he hissed in my ear.

How could my mother stay married to this man? Was my father worse than this? She'd never married him. She never told me about him. I didn't even know his name. But no one could be worse than this awful man.

I couldn't do this again. I was done being scared. Either he would beat me until he killed me, or he would kick me out. I had feared both for so long. My mother had told me once that all men would do in this world was think about sex when they looked at me. I would be used by men my whole life. She was always telling me to leave.

Today I was ready. I only had eight hundred and fifty-five dollars saved up, but I could get a bus ticket to the other side of the country and get a job. If I got out of this house alive, that's what I was doing.

Marco's hands slipped down the front of my shorts, and I bucked against him, screaming. I didn't want his hand there. "Let me go!" I yelled, loudly enough for the neighbors to hear.

He pulled his hand out and jerked me around by my arm so hard it popped. Then he slammed me against the door. His hand punched my face with a loud crack. My vision blurred, and I felt my knees go weak. "Shut up, bitch, and take it."

His hands grabbed my shirt and jerked it up, then tugged my bra down. I sobbed, because I couldn't stop the horror. It was coming, and I couldn't stop him.

"Get away from my husband, you whore, and leave my house! I don't want to ever see your face again!" My mother's voice stopped Marco, and he moved his hands off my breasts. I jerked my shirt back down.

My face was burning from the punch, and I tasted blood on my lip as the stinging cut under my tongue began to swell.

"Out, you stupid, good-for-nothing whore!" my mother screamed.

That moment changed everything.

Mase

Two years later

Fucking hell. What was that noise? I peeled my eyes open as sleep slowly faded from my brain and I registered what had woken me up.

A vacuum? And . . . singing? What the fuck?

I rubbed my eyes and groaned in frustration as the noise got louder. I was sure now that it was a vacuum. And it sounded like a really bad version of Miranda Lambert's "Gunpowder & Lead."

My phone said it was only eight. I had been asleep for two hours. After thirty hours straight with no sleep, I was being awakened by bad singing and a motherfucking vacuum?

As she sang the first two lines of the chorus, I winced. She was getting louder as she sang. And it was seriously off key. That was a good song she was butchering. Didn't the woman know that you didn't come into people's houses at eight in the fucking morning and sing at the top of your lungs?

I was never going to get back to sleep with this racket.

Nannette must have hired an idiot to clean her fucking

house. But then, knowing Nannette, she was pissed because I was here and there was nothing she could do about it. She had probably paid the woman to screech outside my bedroom door. Nannette didn't own the house; our dad, Kiro, did. He'd told us that while Nannette was back in Paris, I could stay at the house and spend some time with our other sister, Harlow, who lived in Rosemary Beach with her husband, Grant, and their new baby.

This must have been the bitch's way of getting back at me for staying at her place.

Now she was singing the chorus over and over again at the top of her lungs. God, it was like waking to a nightmare. This woman so needed to shut up. I had to get some sleep before I went to visit Harlow and her family. She was so excited about me coming all the way from Texas. But this idiot was messing up my sleep very effectively.

I threw back the covers and stood up and headed for the door before I realized I was naked. My head was pounding from lack of sleep, and I was getting angrier as I searched the room for the damn jeans I had taken off when I'd gotten here. My vision was blurry, and the dark curtains were closed. Fuck it. I reached for the sheet and wrapped it around my waist and went for the door.

I swung it open just as she started singing the opening lines to another song. Dammit. Not another song. This time, she was murdering "Cruise" by Florida Georgia Line.

I blinked and rubbed my eyes against the light, my vision still blurry. Shit, did the woman not see me standing here?

After a few seconds, I finally was able to open my eyes in a squint to see a round little ass wiggling as she bent over. My eyes slowly opened wide as I took in the longest damn legs I'd ever seen. And holy fucking hell, her ass. Was that a freckle under her left butt cheek?

She stood up, and her tiny waist only made her ass look better. She continued to shake her bottom as she sang off key. I winced as she hit a very high note. Damn, the girl couldn't sing.

Then she turned, and I hardly had a moment to appreciate the front view before she screamed and dropped the vacuum cleaner as she pulled her earbuds out of her ears. Big, round baby-blue eyes stared at me in horror as she opened and closed her mouth a few times as if she was trying to speak.

I took the moment of silence to check out her full pink lips and the perfect shape of her face. Her hair was pulled up in a bun, but it was the color of midnight. I wondered how long it was.

"I'm sorry," she managed to squeak out, and my eyes went back to hers. She was really something. There was an exotic quality about her. It was like God had picked all the best pieces and put them together to create her.

"I'm not," I replied. *Not anymore. Who the hell needs sleep? Oh, yeah. I do.*

"I didn't know, uh . . . I thought the place was still empty. I mean, I didn't know someone was staying here. There wasn't a car outside, and I rang the doorbell, but no one answered, so I used the code and came on in." She wasn't Southern. Maybe Midwestern. I just knew she wasn't from around here. She lacked the twang of the local accent. There was a softness to her voice.

"I flew in. Had a car drop me here," I said.

She nodded and then looked back down at her feet. "I'll be quiet. I can come back up and do this area later. I'll just go downstairs and start there today."

I nodded. "Thanks."

Her cheeks flushed as she let her gaze drop to my bare chest. Then she turned and hurried away, leaving the vacuum behind in her escape. I watched, enjoying the way her bottom bounced. Damn, I hoped she cleaned several times a week. Next time, I wouldn't be exhausted. Next time, I'd find out her name.

Once she was out of sight, I stepped back into the room and closed the door. A grin tugged at my lips when I thought about her face when she'd realized I was only wearing a sheet. How did Nan have a housecleaner who looked like that? The girl was gorgeous.

I lay back down and closed my eyes. The image of that freckle sitting right there under the plumpness came to mind. I really wanted to lick that freckle. Cutest fucking freckle I'd ever seen.

Reese

"Ohgod, ohgod, ohgod, ohgod," I chanted as I sank down on the nearest sofa and covered my face with my hands.

I hadn't realized someone was staying here. I'd woken him up. He seemed annoyed, I thought. Oh, God, I couldn't tell. I'd been so nervous that he was going to fire me. This was my best-paying job, but I'd never met the owner. I worked for a cleaning service, and they got me the jobs. This was the biggest house I had, and the once-a-week cleaning paid the monthly rent on my apartment and all my utilities and food. The other houses I cleaned were smaller, so if I lost this house, it would take all those other jobs combined to pay my bills. I wouldn't have anything left over to save. No safety net.

The image of his bare chest taunted me, and I closed my eyes tightly, pushing it out of my head. I didn't trust men. Well, except for my neighbor Jimmy. He was the one who had hooked me up with the cleaning service. He liked men, not women, so I felt safe with him.

I also didn't normally enjoy the view of a guy's chest. But that chest . . . well, it was *really* nice. His arms were so thick and corded with muscles. What was I thinking? Yes, his body was beautiful, but men like him who lived in houses like this didn't want someone like me for more than a booty call.

That man was rich and gorgeous and possibly had a woman in bed with him who was just as rich and gorgeous. In fact, I was sure he did. The largest bedroom upstairs had a walk-in closet full of the most beautiful clothing I had ever seen. I figured a woman lived here, and this guy could be her boyfriend. I just wasn't sure why he'd be staying in a different room. But it wasn't my business. So no matter how nice those arms and that chest were, or how chiseled his face was, even with several days' worth of stubble, he was not safe to think about.

I had to make sure I didn't lose this job. The place was usually pretty clean, because no one had lived here in the months since I'd been working, but I cleaned it weekly like it was filthy. No dust could be found anywhere, and I even went as far as organizing the pantry and the cleaning closet, scrubbing the cabinets and throwing out any expired food.

Standing up, I shook off my humiliation at having woken up the client by singing God knows how loudly and vacuuming right outside his door. When he saw how clean everything was, maybe he'd overlook my mistake.

✠

Three hours later, the downstairs was immaculate. I had even wiped out the fridge and the freezer completely again, giving the client plenty of time to sleep. I went to the second floor and cleaned every room thoroughly until I couldn't find anything else to clean, before I finally stood at the foot of the stairs and looked up to the third floor. It was one in the afternoon, and he was still in bed. I had three bedrooms and three full bathrooms to get to, plus a theater and a game room with a full bar. The game room was far enough away from his room that, if I was quiet, I could probably clean it without waking him.

I tiptoed up the stairs and eased past his room. When I was safely in the game room, I let out a sigh of relief. I closed the door behind me and turned to face the large, untouched room. The bar was stocked with every alcohol imaginable and so many different glasses I couldn't even begin to figure out what went with what. I walked across the room and set my basket of cleaning supplies down on the floor. I decided today I would spend some extra time cleaning the windows. I grabbed a chair and covered it with a clean cloth before standing on it. The ceiling was at least twelve feet high, which made the windows hard to reach. Sometimes I brought a ladder in here, but it would make too much of a racket if I tried to bring it up today.

I had reached up with a cloth to begin scrubbing the windows from top to bottom when my cell phone rang. *Crap!* I always put the ringer on high when I was working so I could hear it around the house. I scrambled to get down, but my foot slipped. I winced in pain just before the chair turned over, and my arms shot out to grab for the closest thing next to me. A massive, ornate mirror.

The sound of breaking glass came just before my butt hit the floor with a resounding thud.

And my stupid cell phone was still blaring at top volume.

I turned and desperately reached for my phone but couldn't grab it. The loud ringing continued as I wiggled over to it, my legs all twisted up.

The door swung open, and I froze in place.

Here I sat, with shattered glass all around me and an up-turned chair. The only bright spot was that my phone had finally stopped ringing.

"What the hell happened? Are you OK?" he asked, as he stalked toward me in a pair of white boxer briefs. At least he wasn't totally naked. I jerked my eyes away from him and his almost-naked body and sucked in a breath. I'd broken his mirror and woken him up again.

"I'm so sorry. I'll pay you back for the mirror. I know it probably costs a lot, but you don't have to pay me until it's covered. I'll even come in more than once a week for free."

He frowned, and my stomach dropped. He wasn't happy. "Are you bleeding? Shit, give me your hand."

He dropped to his knees and took my left hand in his. Sure enough, there was a piece of glass in it, and blood was slowly trickling out around the shard.

"You're gonna need stitches. Let me put on some clothes, and I'll take you to the hospital," he said, standing back up and heading for the door.

I stared down at the glass and back up at the door. He was taking me to get stitches. For this? If my cleaning agency found out, they would fire me themselves. I couldn't let him make a big deal out of it. I just needed some peroxide and something to wrap it up. Then I would clean up the mess I'd made.

I stood up and winced from the pain in my backside. I was going to have a bruise for sure. I dusted off the few slivers of glass still clinging to my clothes, but they opened up tiny cuts in my fingers. The blood that smeared down my legs only made things look worse than they were.

I eased out of the wreckage I had created. Once I was sure

I wasn't trailing any pieces of glass after me, I found a clean cloth in my basket, then went to the nearest bathroom to the right of the game room, wet the cloth, and cleaned up my legs.

"What are you doing?" His voice sounded mad.

I jerked my head up and backed away as he filled the doorway of the bathroom. My foot was up on the closed toilet seat lid, and I immediately dropped it back to the floor. "I'm sorry I'm barefoot. I was going to clean the toilet lid once I was done."

His frown grew. Crap. I wasn't making this better.

"I don't care about the fucking toilet. Why didn't you wait for me to help you up? You could have stepped in more glass."

What? This time I frowned. I wasn't understanding him. "I was careful," I replied, still not sure what had him upset.

"Come on. I'm going to pull that glass out and clean the wound and wrap it before we leave. You can't keep it in there. It could get infected."

"OK," I replied, afraid to tell him no. He was obviously intent on helping me.

He turned and started walking out, so I followed him. I only glanced down once at his bottom, and that was only because I was curious about what his backside looked like in those jeans he was wearing. It was just as impressive as his front. Those jeans fit nicely.

I sent my gaze up his back and noticed for the first time that he had a ponytail. His hair wasn't that long, but it seemed at least to hit his shoulders. I hadn't allowed myself to look at him enough to notice. His eyes and strong jawline had taken all my attention before.

We reached his bedroom door, and he stood back and

waved me inside. "I have no idea where Nan keeps her first-aid supplies, but I've got some in my duffel. I'm doctoring a fall from a horse I'm breaking, so I came prepared."

Nan? Who was Nan? "Do you not live here?" I asked.

He pulled out a small blue pouch from his camouflage duffel bag and turned to look back at me. A grin lifted the corners of his mouth, and his eyes danced with amusement. "Hell, no." He chuckled. "Have you met Nannette? No one willingly lives with her. But since our father owns this house, I can stay here whenever I choose. I just choose to do so when Nan is gone."

"Oh. I've never seen anyone here until you," I said.

"That explains a lot," he mumbled, then chuckled as if he knew a joke I didn't. He held out his hand. "Here, give me your hand. I will be as gentle as I can, but this is gonna sting."

I didn't let men touch me. But something about the concerned way he was studying my palm made me trust him. He was a nice guy, or he seemed to be a nice guy. He wasn't looking at me in ways that made me nervous.

I placed my hand palm up in his, and he glanced up at me apologetically, as if it was his fault. I watched as he slowly slid the glass out of my palm and then began dotting it with a cotton ball he'd coated in peroxide. Yes, it stung, but I'd been through much worse.

He bent his head and started gently blowing on my wound as he cleaned it. The cool feel of his breath on my skin eased the sting, and I became fascinated with the way his lips looked puckered up. Was he for real? Had I hit my head when I fell? Was this some strange dream?

He held the cotton ball tightly against the wound, pressing

it down with his thumb while he reached for a new cotton ball and medical tape. "I wish I had some salve for it, but I rarely use it, so I didn't bring any. I've got some Tylenol you can take to ease the pain until we can get you to the hospital."

I just nodded. I didn't know what else to do. No one had ever cared that I had an injury. And I'd had many.

"My name is Mase, by the way," he said, as he glanced up at me while wrapping my hand.

"I like that name. I've never heard it before."

He chuckled. "Thanks. Do you have a name?"

Oh. He was asking what my name was. No one I had worked for had asked me my name except for one client. But she was different from the clients at the other places I worked.

"Yes, I do. It's Reese."

Mase

She smelled like a fucking cinnamon bun. That sweet cream icing and cinnamon smell that made your mouth water. Not taking deep whiffs as her scent wafted over me was hard. But I managed not to act like a psycho and pull her up against me so I could bury my face in her neck and just breathe. I'd never known a woman to smell like a cinnamon bun, but damn, it was a turn-on.

I got her hand wrapped up and then led her down the stairs. She seemed confused about something, but she didn't say much. I asked her if she had a purse, and she nodded and went to get it from the table beside the door. It wasn't what most women would call a purse; it was a faded blue backpack. She slung it over her shoulder and looked back at the house with a worried expression.

"I'm not done cleaning," she said, then looked back at me.

"You can't clean with your hand torn open," I pointed out, unable to suppress a grin.

Her brow puckered into a frown. "It isn't that bad. I can work like this," she said, holding up her bandaged hand.

I shook my head and opened the door. "No, you can't."

We stepped outside and saw that my truck had arrived. I had been waiting for someone to drop it off. Good, I could drive it instead of her car.

"Where's your car?" I asked her.

"I don't have one."

"Did someone bring you?" I asked, already knowing her answer would be that her boyfriend had brought her. Fuck.

"I have a neighbor who works at the Kerrington Country Club. I ride with him, and then I walk here from there."

A neighbor. "He doesn't bring you here?"

She shook her head and looked at me like I was crazy. "No. It's like a mile away. I enjoy the walk."

"Who's your neighbor?" I ask.

"His name is Jimmy."

I was going to have a talk with Jimmy. It wasn't safe for someone who looked like her to be walking around by herself. Rosemary Beach was a safe place, but there were people who drove through going from one town to the next. "Does Jimmy take you home?"

She glanced at me with uncertainty. Like she wasn't sure she should answer me. "Sometimes—yes, most of the time."

Why didn't she have a car? She had to be twenty-one or twenty-two. She wasn't a kid. She had a job and an apartment, I would assume. "How do you get home when Jimmy doesn't give you a ride?" I asked, holding the truck door open for her. I held out my hand for her to take with her good one and helped her into the truck cab.

"I walk," she replied, not looking at me.

Fucking hell.

Glancing down at her cheap flip-flops, I noticed that she

had perfect little pink-tipped toes. Even her feet had to be sexy? Damn.

She tucked her feet back, and I knew she had seen me looking at them. I closed the truck door and took my time walking around to the driver's side. This girl needed help, but I couldn't save her. I was here for a week, maybe two, before I headed back to Texas. Getting worked up over this girl's problems wasn't smart.

My cell phone started ringing in my pocket before I could start the engine, and I knew it was Harlow. She was expecting me at around two. Glancing at the clock, I saw it was almost two now.

"Hey," I said into the phone, as I cranked up the truck and headed toward the main road.

"Did you get some sleep?" she asked. I could hear Lila Kate, her baby girl, fussing in the background.

"Uh, yeah," I replied. I couldn't tell her how little sleep I'd gotten, since the reason was sitting beside me.

"You still coming at two? Grant said he'd give us an hour and then he'll be here by three."

I glanced over at Reese's injured hand. That was going to take a while. An ER waiting room was never fast. "There was an accident this morning. The girl who cleans Nan's house fell and sliced her hand open. I'm taking her to get stitches. Could be a while before I get there."

"Oh, no!" Harlow said, her voice filled with concern. One of the many reasons I preferred Harlow to Nan. "Is she OK?"

She hadn't even winced when I cleaned her with peroxide. Hell, I even winced when I had a cut like that. "Seems to be. Just a nasty cut. She doesn't have a car, and I'll need to take her home afterward. Might be later on tonight before I get there. But you've got me the rest of the week. You'll be sick of my face before Sunday," I assured her.

Harlow laughed. "Doubt it, but that's fine. Take your time. Get her fixed up and safely home. I'll take a nap with Lila Kate. She was up a lot last night. She's teething."

"Get some sleep, then, sweetheart. I'll see you tonight," I replied, before ending the call.

"You don't have to stay with me. I'll get a cab to take me home," Reese said.

I wasn't leaving her to get stitches and take a cab home. Did I look like the kind of jackass who would do that? "I'll stay with you," I said firmly.

"Really, it's very nice of you to take me. But I've had cuts worse than this before. I don't even need stitches. I can just finish up cleaning and head home."

What? Was she serious? "You're getting stitches, and I'm taking you home." I was frustrated and getting pissed. Not at her. God, who the hell could get pissed at someone who looked like her? But I was pissed that she seemed to think it was OK not to get stitches.

She didn't argue this time. I glanced over at her, and she was sitting straighter, and her body was leaning toward the door as if she was trying to get away from me. Had I scared her?

"Look, Reese, you were cleaning my sister's house, and you got hurt. It's our responsibility to make sure you are prop- erly taken care of. I'm not going to let you finish cleaning the house today or even tomorrow. You can come back once your hand is better and it doesn't hurt. I'll be here all week, and I clean up after myself, unlike my sister. I don't need a house-cleaner."

She didn't look at me, but she nodded.

It looked like that was the only response I was going to get. Fine. She could pout about this, but seriously, all I'd done was demand that she let me take care of her. What was her deal?

Reese

This day could not get any more humiliating. Mase had turned up the radio for the rest of the ride to the hospital. He hadn't said another word. I knew he was either angry or frustrated. I was keeping him from a woman, but I'd tried to let him go. He just wouldn't listen to me.

Once we were at the ER, he got me a soda while we waited, even though I told him I didn't need one. By the time they took me back for stitches, we had said all of five words to each other. I wanted to tell him to leave again and that I'd get a cab, but I was afraid he'd snap at me. I didn't know this man. I had no clue what he was capable of.

When they had given me a shot, Mase had held my other hand and told me to squeeze if I needed to. What did that even mean? Was he trying to ease the pain? It was just a shot. When they had stitched up my gash, which needed five stitches, he had continued to hold my hand.

He had told me jokes. They were corny, but I'd laughed. I didn't think anyone had ever tried to make me laugh before. I knew it was the first time I'd ever been told a joke that wasn't about me. In school, I had heard enough jokes, but I had been the butt of them all.

Now he was pulling up in front of my apartment. He hadn't spoken to me during the entire drive. He'd looked like he was going to say something more than once, but he'd stopped himself. Eventually, he'd turned up the radio again, and I knew that meant he was done talking to me.

I couldn't be hurt over his silence. He had put off his date or girlfriend to take me to the hospital and get stitches. During the whole thing, he had been so nice—more than that, actually, he had been kind. But now his mind was on his sweetheart, the girl who was waiting for him.

I had been called "babe," "sugar," and "hot momma" in the past, which still made me cringe. I had also been called other less desirable names, but never "sweetheart." I wondered what that must feel like. To have someone speak to you that way and mean it. To know he wasn't going to hurt you.

When he parked the truck, I knew I had to thank him again and send him on his way.

"Thanks again for taking me, and for the soda, and for . . . for, um, holding my hand. I really appreciate it. I'm sorry I ruined your day. And I'll be back to clean up on Sunday. I don't have another house booked for that day. And you're leaving then . . . right?"

Mase sighed and looked at me. "Yeah, I'm heading home Sunday. At least, that's the plan right now. But don't worry about the house until your hand is better. Nan won't be back for another month. She's in Paris."

Paris. Wow. I couldn't imagine going somewhere like Paris. I wondered what this Nan looked like. If she was his sister, I imagined she was beautiful.

"OK, thanks," I said again, unable to stop thanking him. I grabbed my backpack and opened the truck door.

"Wait. Let me help you down," Mase said, stopping me. He had done this every time I got into or out of the truck. It was as if he didn't think I could just hop down on my own without hurting myself. But then again, after what he had witnessed today, he probably thought I was a klutz.

He was in front of me, holding out his hand again for me to take. I let him help me, because I was sure it was the last time I'd see this man. He didn't realize it, but he'd given me hope. And he'd shown me that not all men were evil.

I bit my tongue to keep from thanking him again. Instead, I just nodded and headed for apartment 1C.

"Reese," Mase called out, stopping me in my tracks.

I turned to look back at him. The sun was setting behind him, and I was sure nothing had ever been quite that perfect in all of history.

"You didn't ruin my day," was all he said before opening his truck door and climbing back up.

I wanted to watch him drive away. But I didn't.

✠

The next morning, my hand was throbbing. But I took the antibiotic and pain medicine the doctor had given me and got ready for work. I had another house to clean that day in Rosemary Beach. Jimmy had gotten me this one, because he was friends with the owners. I wasn't about to let him down and call in sick.

Jimmy was standing outside my door with two to-go cups

of cappuccino, smiling. He wasn't just nice, he was gorgeous. And he knew it. It was odd that I didn't think of him as a regular guy, though. He was more like my very first girlfriend. I'd told him that once, and he'd cackled with laughter.

He also had a cappuccino machine in his apartment. I was beginning to love that machine.

"Good morning, gorgeous. Here's your wake-up juice," he said, handing me the cup. I started to reach for it with my bad hand and stopped. I used my good hand, but Jimmy's eyes were already locked on my bandaged one. "Girl, what the hell happened to you?"

I sighed, hating to remember the mess I'd made yesterday. "I fell while cleaning a window, broke a mirror on the way down, and sliced open my hand." I didn't want to give him details. I held up the bandaged hand. "Five stitches. The owner's brother gave me a ride to the hospital."

Jimmy winced. "Ouch. You sure you can clean a house today? That's got to hurt."

"I'm fine. I'll be a little slower, but you can bet I won't be standing on chairs anymore to clean windows," I joked.

He didn't grin, just shook his head. "You are one piece of work, Reese Ellis. Come on, let's get your hot ass to the Carters'. I also have a number for you to call. Blaire Finlay is a close friend of mine, and she's interested in hiring a new housecleaner. The one she has now is retiring, and she wants someone young. She's got a little tike. It was getting hard for their cleaner to handle his messes. Kid's cute as a button, though." I took the number he handed me. "Call her. She's a doll. You'll love her."

Another job I was getting without using the agency. This

was good. I got to keep all the income from clients I found on my own. "Thanks, Jimmy," I said, tucking the number into my pocket. "I'll call her once my hand is better. I don't want to show up at her house with a bandaged hand."

Jimmy grinned, and his angel face showed even brighter. "She's actually Harlow Carter's sister-in-law, for all intents and purposes."

That didn't really make sense. What did he mean, for all intents and purpose? I figured it didn't matter. Besides, I really liked Mrs. Carter. She was there often when I cleaned, because she had a baby, so I had spoken to her several times. She always tried to get me to stop and have lunch with her. I was sure I'd be happy working for her sister-in-law, too.

"I have to work a fund-raiser benefit tonight at the club. I won't be done until one in the morning. Wish you'd take a cab home. Especially with that bum hand of yours. After cleaning at the Carters', you're going to be tired. And probably hurting."

We had this discussion every day when he had to work late. He always wanted me to take a cab home, but we lived only eight miles from the club, right outside Rosemary Beach and back a few roads inland. I had walked to school, the library, and the grocery store my entire life. I was used to walking to get to places. If I wanted to go somewhere, I had to walk.

I could probably afford a car now, but I couldn't pass the written test. I had asked my mother to help me once, and it had been a terrible mistake. She'd made sure I understood that lazy, stupid people shouldn't drive cars. It was dangerous to everyone else. I had tried twice now to read the study guide for the written test, but it was no use. The words never made sense to me.

Which was how I knew that my mother and my stepfather and all the kids at school had been right: I was stupid. I had to be. My brain didn't work the way everyone else's did. I was twenty-two, and I still went to the library and got picture books and tried to read them.

"I bet Harlow would give you a ride after work, if you'd just ask her. Hell, I'll ask her. People don't get any sweeter than Harlow Carter."

I was not asking her to drive me home. "It's OK. I'll think about calling a cab. I promise," I told him, knowing that I would think about it but wouldn't do it.

Mase

I hadn't gone to Harlow's last night. I'd gone back to the house and cleaned up the glass, then called and explained that I was exhausted. I still had sleep to catch up on. The few hours I'd gotten that morning weren't enough.

When I'd woken up to silence this morning, I'd felt an odd sense of loss. Which was odd, considering that Reese couldn't sing for shit. I didn't plan on seeing the girl again. Even if I didn't leave on Sunday, I wouldn't be here when she got here. I had an urge to fix all her problems. Which was stupid. She was doing fine without me. But something about those big eyes . . . and hell, who was I kidding? There wasn't a part of her body that didn't scream for attention. And I wanted to give her that attention.

A woman like that should have a man. Made no sense why she didn't.

I pulled up outside Harlow's and pushed all thoughts of Reese out of my mind so I could move on from yesterday. Yes, I thought I deserved a motherfucking trophy for *not* kissing those plump lips, but that was over now.

The front door swung open, and Harlow came running out, grinning like a little girl. In my head, she'd always be my baby sister. I could still see her pigtails and the gap between her two front teeth as she smiled up at me. She'd had freckles on her nose back then, too. She'd needed me for a long time, and I'd taken care of her. But Grant Carter did that now.

"You're here!" She squealed and threw herself into my arms.

I chuckled at her enthusiasm and held her in my arms as she kissed my cheek. "Sorry I didn't make it yesterday. Long day," I said, feeling guilty for not coming by last night.

"It's OK. I have a full day planned out for us. Lila Kate is sleeping inside, and the housecleaner Grant insisted we need is cleaning upstairs. Which, by the way, don't get me started on that. He didn't like that I was cleaning while Lila Kate was sleeping; he thinks I should be sleeping with her and getting more rest. He doesn't want me cleaning the house." She rolled her eyes as if he was ridiculous. But I agreed with him. Harlow had a heart condition that had almost taken her from us. The memory of nearly losing her during childbirth was still too raw. Lila Kate had been several days old before Harlow had opened her eyes.

"He's right," I replied simply, and Harlow laughed at me.

"Come on in. I have brunch ready. I've been watching the Food Network while giving Lila Kate her bottle in the middle of the night, so I've been into cooking lately. It started an itch."

I followed Harlow inside as she chatted happily. Hearing the joy in her voice and seeing the love shining in her eyes made me really like Grant Carter. I wasn't sure at first, but the dude had won me over. He made my little sister happy. He adored her the way she needed to be adored.

"I'm back inside, Reese. You don't have to keep an eye on Lila Kate. I have the monitor with me. Thank you!" Harlow called up the stairs.

Just as the name "Reese" was sinking in, I looked upstairs to see those baby-blues staring down at me, all wide and surprised. Well, shit. So much for not seeing her again.

"Reese, this is Mase, my brother. Mase, this is Reese. She's the best housecleaner in the world. I have Jimmy to thank for pointing her my way."

I saw her cover her bandaged hand with her good one as she forced a tight, nervous smile. She was working with her hand like that. Dammit. Did she not listen to anything I had said? She was so fucking stubborn. Her stitches had to be burning like a motherfucker.

"She's pretty dedicated, too, since she's cleaning your house with five fresh stitches in her palm. Your pain tolerance is really impressive, Reese," I said.

"What?" Harlow gasped. "Oh! Reese cleans Nan's, too?" Harlow swung her gaze up to Reese. "You're cleaning after slicing your hand open yesterday? Why didn't you tell me? I would have never expected you to come in today. You need to rest your hand. You could tear it back open," Harlow scolded her.

I watched as Reese straightened her shoulders and stuck her bandaged hand behind her back, as if that would make it go away. "I'm fine. Really, I am. I woke up this morning, and it didn't hurt at all. Well, maybe a little, but I took my medicine, and it was better. I'm almost done with the upstairs. I won't be but another three hours."

Harlow shook her head. "Absolutely not. You come eat brunch with us, and then Mase can drive you home. I don't want you back here until next week at the earliest. You can't work with your hand like that."

I could see the frustration in Reese's face, but she wasn't going to argue with Harlow. "OK. Let me just put the folded towels in your bathroom, and then I'll be down."

Damn, woman. "The towels are fine wherever they are. Harlow can put her towels away. Come downstairs." It sounded like an order. But she was pushing my patience.

She nodded stiffly and came down the stairs slowly. She wasn't wearing shorts today. Instead, she had on leggings that ended just below her knee. They hugged her like a glove. I wished her damn shirt wasn't so big so I could see her ass in those things.

"I'm sorry he sounds so bossy. He's always been bossy. It's this alpha-male thing he has going on," Harlow said, as Reese stopped in front of us. "Come on, let's go eat. I'm serving some things I just tried for the first time. I can't wait to hear what y'all think about them."

I watched as Harlow walked to the kitchen and waited until she was far enough ahead before looking at Reese. "Let me see your hand," I said softly, trying to ease her tension. It was clear I made her nervous when I was frustrated.

She started to argue. I could see it in her eyes, but she relented and held out her hand to me. I unwrapped it gently and took in the pink, puckered skin. It wasn't infected, but it was abused from cleaning. She needed to put some ice and salve on it.

"I'm getting you some ice. Come on," I told her, holding her wrist and pulling her to walk in front of me.

"I really wish you wouldn't. Harlow will feel bad that I cleaned her house today."

She was worried about Harlow. Why did this not surprise me? "It's fine. Harlow will want you to take care of yourself."

She walked into the kitchen and over to the table, where Harlow was motioning for her to sit.

My relaxing visit with Harlow had just become something different altogether. I walked to the freezer and fixed a bag of ice. Harlow had sat down at the table across from Reese, but I could feel her eyes on me. My sister was reading more into this than there was.

Reese

This was so awkward.

Harlow was the "sweetheart" he had talked to yesterday. That much I had figured out. She'd mentioned him not being able to make it to see her last night. Which I felt terrible about. And now, here I was again, interrupting their visit. Mase obviously adored his sister, and she felt the same way about him. I had no siblings and no clue what that must feel like.

"Kiro called you?" Mase asked, looking at his sister before taking a bite of the sandwich on his plate.

She smiled tightly and nodded. "Yeah. He's having a hard time being away."

"I'm surprised he made it this long. You going to visit your mom?"

Harlow frowned and stared down at her plate. Something was definitely wrong. Did she have mom issues like I did? And he had said "your mom." Did they have different mothers? "He's worried that I could upset her without him there. He thinks it's best for me to wait until he's back."

Mase let out an aggravated grunt. He didn't seem pleased with her answer. He swung his gaze over to me. "You good? The ice helping?"

I nodded.

"Let's not talk about Dad right now. It's rude to talk about family stuff when we have a guest with us," Harlow said, with a smile that didn't meet her eyes. Something Mase had said had bothered her.

"Your dad has a cool name," I said, hoping to ease some of the tension that had suddenly entered the room. "The only Kiro I've heard of is Kiro Manning. I've never heard of anyone else with that name."

Harlow and Mase looked at each other, and then a real smile broke out across Harlow's face, and her eyes danced with laughter. "I've never heard of anyone else with the name Kiro, either. Except, of course, Kiro Manning."

I had started to agree politely when her words slowly sank in. *No . . . wait. No . . .*

"I guess I didn't tell you my whole name when I introduced myself," Mase said with a smile.

OK, wait. I wracked my brain. There had been some news or something around the time I left home about Kiro Manning's wife and daughter. I didn't always have access to TV back then.

"You don't watch much TV, do you?" Mase said with a teasing grin, as he took a drink of his soda.

I wasn't about to explain to him why I didn't watch much TV. I just shook my head. "No, not much, ever."

Harlow sighed and then laughed softly. "Someone who doesn't know who I am, and now you've ruined it, Mase."

I could tell she was joking. I just smiled and tried to wrap my head around the fact that I was sitting at a table with Kiro Manning's children. In what universe did that happen? The awkward feeling skyrocketed, and I wanted nothing more than to get away. I wasn't just interrupting a family gathering, I was interrupting a legendary rock star's family gathering. Oh, God, this was so embarrassing.

I looked at both of them sitting there, so nice, with their easygoing smiles. They seemed like any normal, happy family. They didn't appear to be what you would expect from a rock legend's kids.

"I need to go. I . . . my hand is starting to bother me, and I left my medicine at home. Thank you so much for brunch, and I promise to work overtime next week. You two enjoy the rest of your meal, and I'll see myself out," I said quickly, before either of them could interrupt me. Then I stood and flashed them one more smile before leaving the room as calmly and quickly as I could.

I had just stepped outside when I felt a large hand wrap around my upper arm. "Not so fast. You want to leave, I'll take you. You're not walking."

Mase wasn't holding my arm tightly enough to make me panic, but the firm grip caused my heart rate to spike. I didn't like to be grabbed. I managed to control my reaction. "I, uh, fine. OK. Thank you." It was exhausting to argue with this man. He was going to win. I might as well give in.

He seemed pleased that I wasn't going to put up a fuss. He dropped his hand and placed it on my back, as if to lead me toward his truck. I walked ahead of him fast enough so that his hand couldn't rest against me. I didn't like to be touched. Not like that, especially. Even though reminding myself how much I didn't like to be touched wasn't making the warm, tingly feeling on my back where his hand had been go away. It wasn't an unpleasant sensation, just a new one. A very new one. Like, it had never happened until now.

Mase opened the truck door before I could reach for the handle, and he took my hand to help me up. Once again, I was in his truck, but this time, I knew more about him. That he was a good, well-loved brother. That he adored his sister. That he was Kiro Freaking Manning's son.

Holy crap, that was insane.

When he was behind the wheel, I glanced over at him. His tall, muscular body was covered in a flannel shirt and faded, worn-out jeans. His thighs filled the jeans out well, and I could see the muscles flex.

"When you get home, put some of that salve on your wound that we got yesterday. It'll soften the skin around it and ease the pain."

"I will," I assured him.

He nodded and reached for some sunglasses he had tucked into the sun visor and put them on. How did one look sexy while putting on sunglasses? Until that moment, I wouldn't have thought it was possible.

"Do you need to call Jimmy and let him know you got a ride home?"

I shook my head. "No, I was walking home anyway. He has to work tonight."

Mase scowled. "There is cab service around here, you know."

I picked at the bandage and kept my gaze down. I didn't want to give this man my life story to explain why a cab was pointless. I liked walking. It was what I'd always done.

Mase sighed when I didn't respond. "Are you working tomorrow?" he asked.

I didn't have a house to clean tomorrow. It was the day I went to the library and exchanged my books. I would take a walk on the beach and clean my apartment and buy groceries. It was my time for me. "No. I don't work tomorrow."

"Good."

Mase

Two days after I took Reese home from Harlow's, I was still wondering about her. Worrying about her damn hand and her walking everywhere. I was trying like hell to shake it. She wasn't my responsibility.

Harlow handed me Lila Kate after she rescued her from her car seat. I held the little miracle baby close in my arms, because she was still so stinking tiny. And the way Grant hovered over her like she might break made me think she just might. I was careful.

"You carry her. I'll get the diaper bag," Harlow said, reaching for the large bag full of Lila Kate's traveling supplies. The bag was bigger than the baby.

"We're just going to meet the Finlays for lunch. She really needs all that stuff for the whole two hours we're gone?" I asked, wondering how it was possible that Lila Kate required a bag that big.

Harlow just grinned and put the strap over her arm, then locked up the expensive SUV our father had given them when Lila Kate was born. "Let's go."

I followed Harlow toward the entrance. "Why didn't we just use the valet?" I asked, thinking it would have been easier.

"Because it takes a while to get Lila Kate and all her stuff loaded. I hate holding up the line."

I glanced at the valet, and there was no one there. I didn't comment, though.

"Good afternoon, Mrs. Carter, Mr. Manning," the guy at the door said, as he opened it wide for us to enter.

I wasn't a member of the Kerrington Club, but Harlow, Rush, my father, Rush's father, and, of course, Nan were all members. I think people assumed I was, too.

"Mrs. Carter, Mr. Finlay and his wife are already seated in the back room. You've been given privacy," the hostess said, before we even reached her. We followed her through the dining room into a room with three glass walls overlooking the gulf and tennis courts.

Blaire stood up immediately and made her way to me. She wasn't coming for me, though. That much I knew.

"Give her to me." Blaire all but squealed, holding out her arms for Lila Kate.

"Hey, Mase!" Nate Finlay said, as he stood up on his chair and waved at me. The kid looked more and more like his father every time I saw him.

"Hey, little man." I walked over to give him a fist bump.

"B'whoa it up. Like dis," Nate said. Then he made a sound with his mouth like something was, in fact, blowing up, and opened his fist.

"That's an Uncle Grant thing," Blaire said, laughing.

I made sure to blow it up and took the seat across from Nate and Rush.

Rush was grinning like Nate was the most entertaining thing in the world. "Sit in the seat. No standing. Remember," he corrected him. Nate plopped down, and Rush ruffled his hair, then looked at me. "Enjoying your visit?" he asked.

"Yeah. It's good to see Harlow doing so well. And happy."

Rush nodded in agreement. "Grant, too. He's always smiling these days."

"Glad I don't live here. You guys look happy and all, but you're falling like dominos. You, Woods, Grant, and now Tripp." I leaned back and grinned. "It's in the water here, so I can't stick around too long. Not ready for that yet."

Rush chuckled and looked over at Blaire, who was cooing at Lila Kate. Blaire was a beauty. No doubt about it. When Rush had decided to settle down, he picked a winner. But still, that wasn't something I wanted. Not yet, at least. I was only twenty-five. Family life couldn't be all fucking roses, the way this bunch made it appear.

"You just haven't met her yet," Rush said, as he looked at Blaire. "When you do, it doesn't matter what you think now. She'll be all you want in life."

I was sure he felt that way, but I worked on a ranch with horses all day. Not much time for women or interactions with females. I was too busy making a living and building on my own land. Sure, I had needs. I was a man. But I had a friend who handled those needs, no strings attached. It worked for us. Cordelia had lived at the next ranch over for most of my life. She and I understood each other.

"Oh, Rush, she's perfect. I think I want a girl. I'm not sure how much longer I can wait," Blaire said, as she kissed Lila Kate's nose.

"Baby, when you're ready for another, I'll make it my number one goal in life to make that happen," he said, with a wink at his wife.

Blaire's cheeks turned pink, and she tried to frown at him but failed.

"Well, looky who they gave me today. I figured it must be VIPs, since I was given the job," a male voice said. I turned to see him smiling at Blaire. He bent over Lila Kate. "Hey, sweetness. You don't have your stingy daddy here today. I might get a turn holding you," he said.

"Hey, Jimmy," Nate called out, and waved. Then he held out his little hand in a fist.

Jimmy knew the drill and blew it up with him. "You want a vanilla Coke, bro?" he asked Nate, who nodded. "What can I get for the rest of you?" Jimmy asked. He walked back to Blaire, took her drink order, and made his way around the table.

When he turned to leave, Harlow called out, "Jimmy, you're friends with Reese, right?"

I snapped my attention to my sister to see what she was about to say. She'd asked me about Reese casually, and I knew she had been digging for the reason behind my helping Reese. But I had ended that. Or so I thought.

Jimmy grinned brightly. "She's my neighbor and my new *Game of Thrones* watching buddy."

"Isn't that the person you mentioned to me about cleaning the house?" Blaire asked.

"Yep. That's the one," he replied.

Harlow looked at Blaire. "She's wonderful. You'll be really pleased with her." Then my sister looked back at Jimmy. "I was wondering about her hand. Is she doing OK?"

Jimmy's smile fell. "She's doing good. She did go to work today, though. I could've beat her sexy ass. But she's a stubborn one. I don't think she has any family at all. Hell, I don't think she has friends. She told me I was her first girlfriend a couple of weeks ago. But then we were sharing a bottle of chardonnay, so it could've been the wine talking. Regardless, she's a good girl. A sweet thing. I can't figure out why she's single. God knows, every hot man in our building has made a pass at her. Even the married ones." He shook his head in disgust.

"That's so sad," Blaire said, looking crestfallen. "Being alone isn't easy. I'm glad she has you."

Jimmy winked at Blaire before turning and walking out of the room.

There was a heavy feeling in my chest. I tried to shrug it off and focus on the conversation around me. But the thought of Reese being alone with no family bothered me. No one but Jimmy was checking up on her. How was that possible? The woman could stop traffic without trying. Hell, she had married men hitting on her.

I would wonder if maybe she was more into girls, but I'd seen her look at my bare chest. I knew better. She hadn't wanted to look, but she'd looked anyway.

When Jimmy came to clean up our plates, I saw Harlow's mind working. She was worrying about Reese, too. "Do you know how Reese is getting home today after work? Are you driving her?" Harlow asked Jimmy.

He frowned and stacked another plate in his arms. "No. She had a smaller house today. She's probably finished by now and heading home."

Harlow turned to look at me. "Would you go find her

and give her a ride? Lila Kate and I can stay here and have dessert."

I was already standing before she had finished asking.

"Reese ain't real good with men. They make her nervous. It's sweet of you to send Mase, but she won't just climb into the car with him," Jimmy said, looking at me warily.

"It's OK. She knows Mase. He took her to get her hand stitched up, and he took her home the other day from my house, too," Harlow assured him.

I watched Jimmy's face as he swung his gaze up to me. His eyes widened, and he grinned. "Well, at least she's got good taste. About damn time," he mumbled.

"Ignore Jimmy. He's a romantic. He will make nothing out of something. Just go give her a ride. Please," Harlow begged. She was worried that I wouldn't go because of Jimmy's comment.

I glanced at Jimmy. "I want to talk to you about her walking. That needs to stop. Drive her to her houses. Don't make her walk from the club."

Jimmy's eyes got big, but I didn't wait around for a response. I knew the rest of them had heard me, and I knew what they were all thinking. But I didn't care. It was going to take more than that to keep me from going to see Reese again. She needed me. Hell, she just needed somebody. And fuck if I didn't want to be there to help her.

This was my mother's fault. She'd raised me to be this way. That was the only excuse I had.

Reese

I didn't notice the expensive-looking SUV pulling up beside me until I heard a familiar deep voice call my name. I stopped and looked over as Mase pulled the car up behind me. I hadn't expected to see him again.

The way my heart picked up its pace and pumped wildly in my chest startled me. What was it about that man that made me feel things I thought were impossible for me?

"Get in," Mase said, as he walked around the front of the vehicle on his way to open the passenger-side door.

Truth was, I didn't want to argue with him. He was here, and I had a chance to be near him for a few minutes. I was going to take it.

I let my eyes quickly take in his jeans-clad bottom and the way the navy-blue T-shirt he was wearing clung to him, unable to hide all that definition. His hair was pulled back, but the curls at the ends made the strands look just messy and tempting to be touched.

When he started to turn back and look at me, I snapped to attention and hurried over to him. "Thanks," I said, as I climbed inside. He didn't help me this time, but then, this car wasn't high like his truck. It was Harlow's car. I knew it looked familiar, but the baby seat in the back was definitely Lila Kate's. I'd seen that before.

Mase closed my door, and I watched in appreciation of all his male beauty as he sauntered around the front of the vehicle, tucking a loose strand of hair behind his ear. The stubble was back on his face today, and I decided I liked him best when he hadn't shaved.

"You worked today," he said, glancing down at my hand. "Your hand feeling better?"

It was. Much better. I hadn't had that much trouble with it today. I'd worn rubber gloves and had been able to clean without it slowing me down. "Yes," I replied. "Were you going somewhere?"

He shook his head and pulled back out onto the road. "No. Just finished lunch at the club. Jimmy mentioned that you worked today and that you were walking home," he explained.

So Mase had run off to come find me? If he'd been going to the Carters', he would have turned a few blocks back. My stomach did a fluttery thing.

Before I could think of anything to say to that, a phone started ringing. Mase leaned back and pulled a flat smartphone from his pocket.

"Hey, everything good?" he said when he answered, looking concerned. "Sure. I'll be back by then. I think I can fit it in. They say how long they need to board?" I tried not to look at his face as he concentrated on the road and the conversation he was having. "Yeah, give it to me," he said, then reached over and opened the glove compartment. "See if there's a pen in there, Reese."

I quickly did as he asked and found a black pen and

handed it to him. He pushed it back at me and picked up a piece of paper sticking up between the seats. "Here, write this down," he told me.

Oh, no. Not this.

He would see what I wrote. And it was hard for me to write things down when they were dictated to me. I had to concentrate. My letters got turned around, and I often started to panic when I felt pressure to write without enough time. I had to be alone, and I needed to focus.

"Three-three-three," he started, and I quickly wrote down the numbers. I could do that. It wasn't hard. "Berkley Road," he added, and my heart began pounding so loudly I couldn't hear anything else. "Fort Worth," he said, before I had even managed to write the B or what I thought was the B. My hands were shaking so badly I wasn't sure I could write anything else.

I sucked in a deep breath and tried hard to get myself under control. Berkley. I had the B. Then it was E. I started to write the E, and it looked like the 3 I had written before. I paused and glanced back at the 3s. Why did they look alike?

His gaze was on me. A cold sweat broke out all over my body, and I forced myself to keep going. It was an R next. I blinked rapidly, as the words I had written twisted and my head began to throb.

"Text it to me," I heard him say. I knew he wasn't talking to me.

I closed my eyes tightly, wanting nothing more than to jump out of the moving vehicle. This was not happening to me. I had lived here almost a year without anyone knowing I was stupid. That stigma had been left behind. I had used the

spell-check on Jimmy's computer to fill out my application for
the cleaning service.

My grip on the pen had turned my knuckles white, and I
looked down at it through the frustrated tears gathering in my
eyes. Now Mase Manning knew just how stupid I was. Of all
people to have figured this out, why did it have to be him? The
universe hated me.

Mase's large hand reached over and took the pen from my
grasp. I let him have it. Then he tossed it into the glove compartment and closed it. I couldn't look at him. He wasn't saying anything, and I refused to meet his gaze. I would see the
pity or, worse, the disgust.

The car stopped, and I sucked in a breath, then reached for
the door handle. I would just bolt. The chances of me seeing
this man again were slim to none. He didn't say anything as I
climbed out of the car. That hurt, even though I was thankful.
He wasn't opening my door or telling me good-bye. He was
just letting me run away like the idiot I was.

I didn't look back at him as I dug for my apartment key in
my backpack.

My hand was shaking so badly I couldn't get the key into
the lock. The tears were blurring my vision, and I let out a sob
of frustration before trying once again to open my front door.

Suddenly, his hand was covering mine, and I watched as
he plucked the key from my weak grasp. I stood in horror and
confusion as he unlocked my door and pushed it open. Why
was he out of the car?

I didn't move. I was frozen in my spot. Then his hand
touched my back, and he gently nudged me inside. Unable to
think for myself, I went. He kept his hand on my lower back

until we were both inside, and the door closed softly behind us. He'd followed me inside. He was going to ask me questions. Questions he already knew the answers to. I had proven in the car how my brain didn't work right. He had seen it first-hand. I just needed him to go away now.

"What happened?" his voice was gentle and kind. There was no ugliness to his question. I almost felt safe. Almost.

Mase

My thoughts were all over the place as I tried like hell to figure out what had happened in the car. I'd never seen anyone do that before. It had been hard to drive as I watched Reese struggle with writing down a simple address. I hadn't realized she was having a problem until she made a soft panicked noise in her throat like she couldn't breathe.

My gaze had gone to her face, and I'd seen she'd gone pale. Glancing down at the paper, I'd also seen three Es instead of three 3s. Her backward B had been enough for me to know something was off. She had to have an explanation. One that made sense.

"I'm stupid . . . I . . . my brain doesn't work right. I went to school for twelve years and still didn't graduate. I can't pass a test. I can't . . . I can't even read. Not much."

Holy shit.

She lifted her hand up to wipe at her tears, and her full lips were puckered up. She was even gorgeous when she cried.

"You're not stupid," I said tightly. I hated hearing her call herself that. Something was wrong with her, but she was not stupid.

She let out a sad laugh and continued to wipe away her

tears. "You may be the first person who knows about this and doesn't think I'm stupid."

My body tensed, and an angry coil tightened in my chest. "Did someone tell you that you were stupid?" I asked, unable to keep my emotions out of my voice. I was pissed.

She stiffened, then glanced at me warily. "Yes," she replied softly.

"Who?"

She studied me a moment. At least my reaction had stopped her tears.

Those big eyes sucked you in, but with them all wet and red from crying, they were more lethal. You wanted to do whatever the hell was needed to make them shine with laughter.

"My parents, teachers, other kids . . . everyone," she replied. "But I am. You just don't know . . ." She trailed off, looking so forlorn and broken. Her tone told me that this wasn't easy on her. I wondered if anyone in her life knew this.

"Then they're the idiots. I've been around you enough to know you're smart. You live on your own and have a job. A stupid person couldn't accomplish all that."

She frowned again, then crossed her arms over her chest as if she were protecting herself.

What kind of parents did this to their child? She must have been a breathtaking kid. The kind people wanted to watch just to see her smile. Hell, I even liked when she pouted.

"Don't tell anyone, please," she whispered, looking up at me.

Did she actually think I'd do that? I ran a hand through my hair in frustration, forgetting that it was pulled back in a ponytail.

I had to help her. I wasn't sure how I was going to manage that, considering I had to go back to Texas in two days. That had been my stepfather on the phone. I was getting more horses to board. And I needed the income. I couldn't not go home in order to handle this.

"I would never do that. But I want to help you," I told her, waiting for her to tell me no and try to make me leave. Instead, her lips puckered up again like she was about to cry. Shit, what had I done now?

"You're so . . . nice. Why are you so nice? I clean your sisters' houses. You don't know me, not really. But you open doors for me, and you don't act like I'm an idiot, and you . . . want to help me?" She said the last bit on a choked sob. "No one can help me. You can't fix what isn't there. And my brain just isn't all there."

Fucking hell. "Don't say that again," I warned her. I was done hearing her demean herself. I had seen intelligence shining in her eyes. "Your brain is fine."

Reese's eyes flashed something I didn't understand, and then a small smile tugged on her lips as she sniffled. "You're really a nice man, Mase Manning. I don't normally like men. They . . . make me nervous. But you, you're different."

My own fucking emotions were too raw for this. I couldn't let myself question why she didn't trust or like men. The haunted look in her eyes when she'd admitted that sent off a warning sign I couldn't miss. She had more secrets—I'd bet my life on it.

Simple fact was, girls who looked like Reese knew men well. They had been controlling them since they hit puberty. Men didn't frighten them. They owned men. Unless . . . No.

I wasn't letting my thoughts go there right now. But God, I hoped I was wrong.

"I have to leave in two days. I'm going back to Texas. I've got business to handle. But I am going to help you. When I'm gone, you can call me, and I'll be there to listen. I'm a really good friend. But I need you to promise me that what I set up for you, to help you, you'll do. You will trust me to put you in good hands. I won't let anyone hurt you. I'm a phone call away."

I wasn't sure what the hell I was going to do in two days, but I had some connections. I was Kiro Manning's son, and sometimes that meant something. I never used it for myself, but I'd use it to help Reese. Kiro could demand the best, and Reese was getting the best.

Reese tilted her head to the side, and I wondered again how long her hair was. How it looked draped across her shoulders. Did it naturally curl, or was it straight?

"Why?" she asked

"Why what?"

"Why do you want to help me?"

I didn't even pause. "Because you're worth helping."

Reese

I stood staring at the door in wonder long after Mase had left.

I didn't understand why he thought I was worth helping, but he did. An unfamiliar feeling of warmth spread through me. I was afraid to move. I didn't want this feeling to vanish. I liked it too much. So I stood perfectly still and enjoyed it.

I was still gripping my phone in my hand. He had taken it from me and added his number to my contacts. He'd even taken a photo of the boots he was wearing so that it would appear on the screen when he called. I wouldn't have to worry about trying to read his name. I would know who was calling.

Smiling, I thought about the selfie Jimmy had taken when he had added his number to my phone. He'd been very into getting a picture of himself. So different from the picture of Mase's boots. I didn't imagine Mase had ever taken a selfie.

I liked Mase Manning. I liked him a lot. Even more than Jimmy. In a very different way. And I knew that wasn't a good thing. Mase was nice to me, but he didn't like me the way I liked him. I could tell by the way he treated me. Maybe that was why I felt so safe with him, because I liked him that way. I knew I'd never have to worry about him feeling the same way. He didn't even live here, after all.

My heart sank.

Shaking my head to clear my thoughts, I put my phone down on the sofa and walked to the kitchen. Getting worked up over this was silly. Mase was going to try to help me, and although I was worried that I couldn't be helped, I had to hope. What if someone could help me? I wanted to believe that. It would change everything. I could do so much more. I could get my GED, and maybe I could even go to college.

With a newfound determination, I picked up my newest picture book from the library and went to curl up on the sofa. I would get through this one today. I could do this. Mase had faith in me. I just needed more faith in myself.

⛒

Three hours later, I was almost finished with my book. My head ached, and my eyes felt red and irritated from straining. The knock on my door was followed by "Yoo-hoo, babe, it's me. I got pistachio ice cream and two spoons."

Smiling, I tucked the book away under the sofa and went to let Jimmy in.

He was smiling a little too brightly when I opened the door. Holding up two spoons, he sashayed into the room as only Jimmy could do and still look good.

I closed the door and turned to look at him.

"I'll admit it now," he said. "This is a bribe. I want to know all about your interactions with Mase Colt Manning. Every last, delicious detail. Indulge me, please. That man stars in several of my fantasies."

A laugh bubbled up out of me. Jimmy winked and sank down on the sofa.

"Spill it, woman," he urged.

I walked over to join him. "I'm afraid you're looking for juicy info that I don't have. Mase has been a nice guy. Nothing to feed your fantasies, I'm afraid."

Jimmy cocked an eyebrow. "Really? Not one little kiss?"

"Uh, no." I sputtered, surprised he would even ask me that.

He dug into the ice cream. "That makes no sense. The man is straight. I'd know if he wasn't. And any straight single man would be on you like white on rice." He paused and let out a sigh. "Damn. That's it. He isn't single. Didn't think about that. Well, crap. I was so hoping you were about to get some action with a piece of Grade A meat."

I cringed and laughed at the same time, but in my stomach, I didn't feel like laughing. I felt a little sick. Or deflated. The idea of Mase having a girlfriend didn't sit well with me. It wasn't like I thought I had a chance or that I even wanted a chance. But he made me feel safe and normal.

"I figured you hadn't dated because you were picky and no one was up to snuff. Mase is up to everyone's snuff, so I thought you'd scored a winner. Sucks to know that ain't the case. Pickings around here are slim. The hotties are getting ticked off the list rapidly." Jimmy took a big bite of ice cream like he was the one who was depressed over this situation.

I had lost my appetite.

"I was so sure, too. He jumped up before Harlow could even get it out of her mouth to go find you and drive you home. The boy didn't even tell everyone good-bye. He just made sure to tell me that he wanted me driving you to your clients. He didn't seem to like you walking. Then he bolted." Jimmy waved his spoon. "Would have bet my left nut he was hot after your ass. And I really fucking like my nuts right where they are."

On that note, I decided to take a bite of ice cream.

"There you go. Eat the creamy goodness, and let's talk about maybe you and me double-dating. My man has a cousin who is *fine*. He lives about an hour away, but he is pretty damn close to Grade A." I started to open my mouth to stop him, but he held up his hand and made a tutting sound at me. "Not so fast. Let me finish my hard sell here. He's a good guy. I know him, and I would be there with you. I wouldn't let anything happen that you weren't perfectly OK with. He's refined. I think you'd like him. He's doing his clinicals right now, and he hardly has time for a life outside of the hospital. When he does go out, meeting women is still hard for him. He likes to keep his work separate from his personal life. So he needs a date."

A doctor? There was no way I could date a man who was that smart. I couldn't even read the dinner menu. My hands would sweat, and my vision would blur from panic. No, I couldn't. But Jimmy looked so hopeful. I hated this. I hated not being able to say yes. Not being able to meet new people and trust that if they found out, they wouldn't judge me or ridicule me.

"You need to do this, and I would be right there beside you. I don't want to know anything you don't want to share with me, but I know something in your past is bad shit. I can see it in the way you live. I've been close enough and watched you enough. Every damn straight man in this apartment build-ing has tried to get your attention. You flee like the bats of hell are on your heels. So you aren't hiding it from me. I see you. And I think whatever is in your past that's screwing up the present needs to be laid to rest. I'm your friend, Reese. Let's do this together."

This was too much. Two people in one day wanting to help me. And both of them men. A species I thought I'd never trust.

"OK," I said, realizing I had to figure this out somehow. Mase had made me brave today. He might not know his words had been a salve to my wounded soul, but they had been. "But I need to know where we're going to eat before we go." I wasn't going to explain why. I couldn't do that right now. Not yet.

Jimmy beamed at me and nodded. "I can do that. Hell, you can even pick the place. Just so you'll go."

I could look up the restaurant's website and print a copy of the menu. Then I could figure out something on it to order. If I was in the privacy of my apartment and alone, I could focus. Maybe.

Mase

One phone call to Kiro, and I had an appointment the next day with a psychologist with a PhD in learning disabilities only an hour and a half from Rosemary Beach. The man stood up to shake my hand from behind his wide, cluttered desk after pushing his glasses back up his nose from where they had slipped. He didn't seem very thrilled about our meeting. An annoyed furrow sat between his white eyebrows, giving him a pinched look.

"You must know people in high places, Mr. Manning. I, as you can imagine, am a busy man, and my courses are coming to the end of the semester."

As I had guessed, he wasn't happy about this. Knowing Kiro, he'd called the president of the university where this guy taught and had him order Dr. Henry Hornbrecker to meet with me today. "I'm sorry that I've come during a bad time for you. I leave town tomorrow, and there's some business I need handled before I go back to Texas."

The man's time was obviously important, so I wasn't going to waste it. I pulled the piece of paper Reese had left crumpled up on the floorboard of Harlow's Mercedes when she scrambled out in a panic. Every time I looked at it, I remembered her struggle, and it made something inside me ache.

I handed him the paper. "I had asked the person who wrote this to write down Three-three-three Berkley Road. If that person is an adult around the age of twenty-two and struggled to write this much, what do you think that means? Why would she write that? And why would it be so difficult and send her into a panic?"

The doctor frowned down at the paper. "Twenty-two, you say?" he asked.

"Yes, sir," I replied.

"Are you asking me for you or for her? Surely a twenty-two-year-old who suffers this severely has already been diagnosed in school or as a child and knows what her problem is."

He knew what the problem was. My heart sped up. "No, she doesn't know. She couldn't finish high school. She can't pass tests. She's been told she's . . . stupid. But she's not. Not at all."

The doctor muttered a curse and sat back down in his chair, looking at the paper I'd given him. "I thought that by this day and age, our public school systems were more adept at labeling and dealing with learning disabilities. Especially one as common as dyslexia. Tell me, does she read?"

Dyslexia. Fuck me.

I'd known someone with dyslexia in school. He had special classes and a tutor who helped him every day. He ended up graduating with honors. No one had helped Reese, and it had been this simple. A lump formed in my throat, and I pressed my fist into my thighs. Anger, relief, and frustration all coursed through me at once.

"No, she can't read," I replied. "She tries, but she struggles. I need to get her help. Someone who can help her read and write. She struggles daily with things that are so simple to everyone else, and she thinks it's because her brain isn't all there. I will pay whatever price." Fuck, I wanted to roar in protest. It was pure injustice. And neglect.

"I know a professor in Panama City. He is younger, but this is a condition that is near and dear to his heart. His father suffered from the same thing and didn't learn to read or write until he was fifty years old. Astor Munroe has had several adult cases that have ended successfully. He even works at a school for dyslexia in a less fortunate neighborhood pro bono, several afternoons a week. I will give him a call and have him contact you as soon as possible."

A man. Reese didn't do well around men. "Is there a female who can do the same thing? Men make her nervous."

Henry frowned. "I don't know offhand of a woman in that area who can help with someone who suffers as severely or has been as neglected as your friend. But I assure you, Dr. Munroe is a nice man. He'll set her at ease."

Maybe she would let Jimmy go with her. She trusted him. Fuck, I needed to stay. But I couldn't. My life and responsibilities were back in Texas. I had done this much. Now it was up to Reese to take the next step. I couldn't force her.

"OK," I said. "Thank you, sir. I appreciate your taking the time to meet with me."

He nodded, no longer looking as annoyed as he had when I arrived. "She'll need testing to confirm my diagnosis, but from what you've told me and what this says"—he held up the paper I'd given him—"it's dyslexia." He reached for a pad and a pen and slid them to me. "Give me her info and yours. I'll have Dr. Munroe contact you either later today or tomorrow, depending on his schedule."

Reese was going to have a chance. I was going to give her one.

⊞

I waited to call Reese until I had heard from Astor Munroe. Twice I had caught myself about to text her when I realized she wouldn't be able to read a text or text me back, so I stopped myself. Instead, I spent the rest of my day and evening with Harlow, Grant, and Lila Kate at the beach, then went back to Nan's to pack my things. I needed to leave as soon as I got the call from the professor.

Before ten the next morning, Astor Munroe called me and said he was very interested in helping Reese. He even sounded excited and intrigued by her situation. His price wasn't cheap, but he explained that he was fitting her into a very tight schedule. He asked me questions that I didn't know the answers to. She had shared very little of her past with me. I gave him her contact information and told him I would be going to talk to her today. I hoped she would call the professor on her own after I left, but if he didn't hear from her in two days' time, he assured me, he would give her a call.

Reese was home when I called her to ask if I could stop by to talk. Now here I was, back at her apartment door, hoping she would take this chance and use it. I couldn't do any more than this. Even if I wanted to stay and hold her hand, that wasn't possible. I had horses and a ranch to get back home to.

Reese opened the door on the first knock and smiled shyly at me before stepping back to let me in. Her hair was down today. Long, dark, silky layers hung halfway down her back in soft waves. It had curl. Damn, that was better than I'd imagined. I had to clear my throat to calm my instant lust.

"I like your hair down," I blurted out, before I could stop myself.

Reese's cheeks turned pink, and a pleased smile touched her lips. Someone had to have told her that before. "Thank you," she replied softly.

I stepped inside and tore my gaze off her long legs, on complete display in those shorts. Even the brightly striped socks that came halfway up her calves didn't detract from those legs of hers.

"Can I get you something to drink?" Her voice wavered like she was nervous.

"Uh, yeah, thanks," I replied, knowing that I didn't have time to drink anything. I needed to give her the details and get to the airport.

She started walking to the little corner of the room that was her kitchen. "I have orange juice, and I just made some lemonade. Sorry I don't have a large selection," she said, glancing back at me.

"Lemonade sounds good."

She beamed like it pleased her that I wanted to try her lemonade. I watched as she pulled down a glass from the open shelves she had instead of actual cabinets. Everything was neatly arranged. The food shelves were even organized. I needed her to come to my place and do my cabinets. They were a fucking nightmare to find anything in.

Ice clinked in the glass, and I shifted my gaze back to her. She poured me some lemonade, then put the pitcher back into the narrow fridge. There couldn't be much room in that thing.

"When you were in school, did anyone ever mention that you could be dyslexic?" I asked, as she brought me the drink.

She paused in mid-step. Then she continued walking toward me. "No, but I've heard of that. I just don't know what it is, exactly."

I took the glass and sat down on the chair across from the sofa. "The specialist I met with yesterday believes that is what you suffer from. Dyslexia does not mean you are in any way less intelligent than other people. I've been put in contact with a professor who has a PhD in learning disorders. He specializes in dyslexia. He's willing to work with you free of charge after hearing about your problems. His father also was never diagnosed and didn't learn to read and write until he was fifty years old. This is a passion of his now. He wants to help people. He wants to help you."

Reese sank down onto the sofa, looking at me with many emotions crossing her face. But the dominant one was fear. I didn't want her to be scared of this. I wanted to give her hope.

"Tell me what you're thinking," I encouraged her.

She gripped her hands tightly in her lap. "What—what if we find out that's not it, and you went to all this trouble. I might just be stu—"

"*Don't* let me hear you call yourself that again. It infuriates me, Reese. I'm serious. You are the farthest thing from that. I promise you. And if that's not your problem, Dr. Munroe will find out what it is. This is a learning disability. It can be conquered."

She closed her eyes tightly and took a deep breath. I could see her wanting to hope for this. I just had to persuade her to reach out and take it. "He can figure out what my problem is if it isn't dyslexia?" she asked, looking at me with those wide baby-blue eyes that did things to my chest.

"Yes. He can."

She let out a small laugh, then covered her mouth as a sob broke free. I wasn't sure if I should comfort her or wait it out, but then she stood up and launched herself at me. Her arms circled my neck as she slammed against me. All that cinnamon sweetness engulfed my senses. "Thank you . . . I don't even know . . . that's not even enough. I can't find the right words. But just . . . thank you," she said, as she let out another sob, still holding on tightly to me.

I gently wrapped my arms around her and tried like hell not to think about how good her tits felt pressed up against me. She was emotional and thanking me; I was not going to take advantage of this. "You're welcome. I'm glad you're willing to do this. I think you're bound for great things, Reese. You just needed someone to give you a lift up."

She pulled back to look at me and give me a watery smile, then buried her forehead in my chest. "I can't believe you. I don't know why you wanted to help me or what I did to deserve this. I woke you up singing, and I know my singing is horrible and was probably very loud. And I broke your mirror and made a mess that I haven't even cleaned up yet, and I bled on you. I just don't know why all that led to you doing something like this for me. But thank you." She barely stopped for a breath as she let out all her feelings against my chest.

Smiling, I reached out and touched her hair. I had been fighting the urge since I'd walked in and seen that it was down. Just as I'd imagined, it was silky. "You broke my sister's mirror, and I don't much care for Nan. Besides, she can afford to replace it. You never bled on me, just the floor, and I've cleaned up that mess. It's long gone. As for your singing, yes, it's horrible. But there's something about you, Reese, that makes me want to ease that lost look in your eyes."

She went very still in my arms, then loosened her hold on me and pulled back to look at me before she unlatched herself from around my neck and moved away, but only by a few inches. A grin tugged at her lips. "My singing is horrible, isn't it?" Then she laughed. "God, I was so embarrassed when I turned around and saw you standing there." She shook her head. "I can cook better than I sing. I promise. Can I make you dinner tonight? I want to do something for you."

Never had I been upset about getting new horses to board. I liked money, and I needed horses to keep the ranch running. But damned if I wasn't resenting them right about now. "I have to go," I told her.

The light in her eyes dimmed but only for a moment. "That's right. You have to get back to Texas. I forgot."

I nodded. "I have to get to the airport right away."

I stood up, and she backed away, giving us more space. I didn't want her to back up. She took that cinnamon and sugar smell with her.

"Dr. Munroe has your number, but here is his contact information. Call him. He's expecting you to call him. He will only call you if you don't."

She took the paper in my hand and nodded. "I will. Today," she replied.

"Good." I needed to leave, but here I stood, staring at her.

"Thank you, again. Really. I may say this a million more times." Her eyes were bright with new unshed tears.

"You don't have to do that. But I'd like for you to call me after your meeting with him. I will be curious about how things go. Keep me updated."

She beamed at me. "Yes. I can do that."

With one last look at her, I headed for the door. I had to get out of here before I reached out and pulled that shiny hair back over to me so I could smell her cinnamon scent and get tangled in all those silky locks.

"Be careful," she called out to me.

I opened her door, then glanced back at her and winked. "Always."

Reese

My double date had to be postponed. We had set it for Thursday, but Thursday was the first evening that I could meet with Dr. Munroe. I thought about calling Mase and telling him that I had called the professor and set up my first meeting, but he had said to call him after my meeting. I didn't want to bug him.

So instead, I stared at the photo of his boots a lot on my phone.

I had a crush on Mase Manning. It wasn't my first crush. I'd had a couple in high school, but I soon found out that those guys were flirting with me only when no one was around. When they saw me in the halls, they ignored me. I was invisible to them unless they got me alone. Those crushes died quickly, and I stopped paying attention to cute guys. My senior year, the captain of the cheerleading squad caught her boyfriend cornering me outside and got furious. He never spoke to me again, which was a relief, but then, shortly afterward, the entire school was talking about me being a lesbian.

I didn't figure that was a bad thing. I wasn't into girls. Especially the mean vipers I went to school with, but I sure wasn't into any of the guys there, either. So I let them call me names, and I ignored them. Eventually, they moved on to someone else who responded to their cruelty.

Needless to say, it had been a while since I had actually had a real, honest-to-God crush on a guy. My stepfather had made sure that I kept men away at a football field's length. I cringed thinking of the man who had taken my innocence and tainted me for life.

Shoving all thoughts concerning Mase aside, I went to take a shower. Memories of how my stepfather always sent me to scrub my body clean under the hottest water I could stand popped into my head, but at least I no longer threw up when I thought of him. I was getting distance from my terrible past. I was improving.

Wednesday evening, my phone rang just as I pulled the lasagna I'd made out of the oven. I had made an entire pan of it, hoping that Jimmy might want to come over and eat. But he'd called me at around three to let me know he was going out that night since I'd bailed on our double-date night. He was on me about giving him another night that would work, but I couldn't seem to muster the interest. Right now, I was very focused on learning to read.

So I kept coming up with excuses for why I couldn't go.

I dropped my oven mitt and went to pick up my phone. My heart started racing when I saw the cowboy boots on my screen. It was Mase.

"Hello," I said on the third ring.

"Hey. You haven't called me." His deep voice came over the phone, and my toes curled into the carpet.

"Oh, well, I don't go to my first meeting until tomorrow," I explained, really thankful that he couldn't see the silly grin on my face right then.

"Good. You have one scheduled. Did you like him when you spoke to him on the phone?"

I walked over and sat down in the chair he had sat in before he left and pulled my feet up under me. "Yes. He was very nice. He seemed eager to meet with me. He asked me several questions, and after hearing my answers, he said he was positive that I do, in fact, have dyslexia." I had wanted to dance around the room when he'd told me that.

"I'll be available tomorrow evening. Call me when it's over. I want to hear everything."

The fact that he cared so much made my little crush pulse and grow even more. Having a crush on someone like Mase Manning was ridiculous. He probably had a world of women with crushes on him. He was helping me, and it would make him uncomfortable to know how I felt.

"OK. I'll call," I assured him.

"Good. I've got to go. I'm having dinner at my parents'. I'll talk to you tomorrow night."

"OK, 'bye," I replied.

Dropping my phone into my lap, I felt like clapping and squealing. But instead, I got up and went to enjoy some lasagna.

✠

Astor Munroe was not what I had been expecting. When I thought of a professor, I imagined a man with silver in his hair and possibly glasses. Maybe even a little potbelly under his button-up starched shirt.

What I hadn't expected was a man of about thirty-five, with a tall, lanky body, wearing a pair of blue jeans, Nike tennis shoes, and a short-sleeved polo shirt. He wasn't handsome, exactly, but then, I was comparing him with Mase, and that wasn't exactly fair. I wouldn't want to be compared with Harlow. They were the beautiful people. So I shouldn't do that to Dr. Munroe.

His soft brown eyes were kind. He didn't make me nervous at all. The moment I walked into his office, he stood up and, with an easy smile, invited me to have a seat. After every question and request, he assured me that it was all to help me learn. It was obvious that he was excited about the challenge I presented to him. He shared the story of his father's struggle, and I was in awe of how, at twenty-one years old, Dr. Munroe had taught his father to conquer something he had been dealing with his whole life.

But when I got up to leave, he made a comment I didn't understand. I thought about it on the cab ride back home, while the female driver chatted on about her grandkids and how good her chicken and dumplings were.

When I had thanked him for fitting me into his schedule so quickly, he had said I had Mr. Manning to thank for that.

Question was, what did that mean? Had Mase done something to get him to act so swiftly? And if so, what?

Mase

Next time someone knocked on my door, I was going to check out the window first before opening it. I had been waiting for Reese's call when I'd made the mistake of answering a knock at the door. Cordelia, my friend with benefits, came strutting in wearing her skintight jeans and a halter crop top. Her boots clicked on the hardwood floor, and she smirked at me as she moved toward my bedroom.

"You haven't called, and I need a good fuck," she hollered over her shoulder, before pulling the halter top off and tossing it at me with a laugh.

My cock didn't even twitch. *Shit.*

I had hoped this . . . thing I was feeling about Reese wasn't more than just a friendship thing. But fuck me, all I could see was what was wrong with Cordelia. For starters, her belly button was pierced. I used to think that was sexy, but now it seemed she was trying too hard. And her hips didn't flare. When she swayed those nonexistent hips, there was no nice roundness to her ass. It was hardly there.

This wasn't going to work. I'd been friends with Cordelia for years. Two years ago, we had gotten drunk and slept together, so instead of making things awkward, we'd agreed that it was OK. We'd scratch each other's itch when we needed to. Only once had we put a halt to it, when she'd gotten serious for about four months with a guy who turned out to be married. She'd ended it, and we'd gone back to our old ways.

I didn't date often. I wasn't available enough for females. They were needy, and after a couple of failed relationships, I had decided that sex with Cordelia was the fix I needed. But things seemed off now. Something had changed.

And it was me.

Dammit. I didn't have time for this.

"You should have called," I told her, tossing her halter top back at her.

She didn't grab it but let it fall to the ground at her feet. The confused frown on her face didn't bode well. "I never call. I just show up. Same for you," she reminded me.

"I'm waiting for a phone call. It's important. I can't tonight."

She cupped her tits in her hands and pinched the pink nipples. "You telling me a phone call is better than this?"

I knew women well enough not to tell her the truth. So I shrugged. "Tonight's not gonna work. I'm not sure when will work. I've got a busy week ahead of me." In case these feelings that were screwing with my head where Reese was concerned faded, I didn't want to end things with Cordelia. She was a friend, too.

She reached down and snatched up her top and jerked it back on. "Fine. Be an ass. I won't be back, so if you want it, you have to come and get it," she said angrily.

Oh, man. This wasn't why I screwed around with her. Cordelia didn't do drama. She was easy to handle. This was drama. I hated drama.

"Sorry, Cord. I really am. But I have a lot going on right now. It's just not a good time for me. Mentally, I'm not in the game."

She glared at me and slammed the door behind her.

With any luck, she'd sleep on this and be over it tomorrow. I liked Cordelia. I just never liked her for more than a friend. The sex thing was just better than jacking off alone. I needed to apologize to her, but for now, I was glad she'd left without too much of a fuss.

My phone rang. Suddenly, I didn't care about Cordelia anymore.

"Hey," I said, as I held the phone to my ear, anxious to hear Reese tell me about her meeting.

"I hope it's not too late. There was a wreck on Thirty-One A, and traffic was backed up." Her soft voice warmed me through the phone.

"No, it's not too late. Who drove you?"

"I took a cab. There's a lady Jimmy knows who lives near Panama City. She's been working this strip of the beach for about twenty years. We don't have many taxis around here."

She had been with a lady. That made me feel better. A strange man driving her would have made her uncomfortable. I hadn't thought about that. I kept forgetting that she didn't have a car. Wait . . . "Reese, can you drive?" If she couldn't read, she never would have passed her written test to get a license.

"No," she answered.

Another thing that had hindered her life. "Next time I'm in town, I'm taking you out on a back road and giving you lessons. We'll study the written test, too."

WHEN I'M GONE ❖ 75

She was silent a moment. I wondered if she was scared to get behind a wheel. Then I finally heard her shuffle around. "OK. I'd like that."

I would, too. "Tell me about your meeting."

"Dr. Munroe was nice. He's very excited about helping me. I took some tests, and I'm definitely dyslexic. That's it. That's all that's wrong with me. He said my teachers or my parents should have caught it when I was a kid, but somehow it was overlooked or misdiagnosed . . ." She trailed off. I didn't want her thoughts going there. Someone had told her she was stupid, and I knew her parents were part of that.

"When do you start working with him?"

"Monday afternoons, he has to come to Grayton Beach, which isn't too far from here. His mother lives there, and he has dinner with her. He said we could meet at the library in town. Then, on Thursday afternoons, I have to go to his office to do lessons. He thinks I'll read quickly once he helps me learn how to focus on the words. No one has worked with me before the way I need."

She was excited. As she continued, she got louder and talked faster. It was cute. I could imagine her blue eyes twinkling with happiness.

"By the time you come back, I might be able to read to you," she said, and then I heard her nervous laugh like she hadn't meant to say that out loud.

"Why wait until I visit? You can read to me on the phone when you call to tell me about your lessons."

She was quiet again, and I let her play with that idea a moment. I didn't want to make her skittish. But I did want her to be comfortable with me. Even on the phone. "You want me to call after my lessons?" she asked.

"Of course I do. If that's OK. I'd like to know how things go."

"Yes, that's fine. I'm . . . I will do that. And when I'm brave enough, I'll read to you."

Reese

For two weeks, I went to my lessons and called Mase afterward. By the fourth lesson, I realized that I was more excited about hearing Mase's voice than I was about my actual lessons. And that was saying a lot, because I loved my lessons. I loved how strong I felt as I learned to focus on words and decipher what things said.

I would never be a fast or avid reader. Dr. Munroe had told me not to let that get me down. Reading would never be my strong point, but I would be able to do it. This wouldn't hold me back from driving, going to college, or filling out job applications anymore.

At the beginning of our third week, I was all set to meet Dr. Munroe at the library in town. He was going to send me home with a book to practice on. The last two books he had given me were very simple, one or two words a page, picture books. I had read those in five minutes each by my next lesson. He was going to give me something more complicated tonight. I was preparing myself for it. I could do it.

Then I would get to call Mase afterward and tell him about my lessons.

⌗

Lila Kate woke up from her nap and cried out, and I moved from the stairs where I was dusting to call for Harlow, but she was already coming running around the corner with a grin on her face. She kept a baby-monitor device on her whenever she wasn't with Lila Kate. I'd forgotten about that.

"She let me finish the cookies I was making for Grant," Harlow said, as she passed me on the stairs. "When they cool, why don't you take a break and have cookies and milk with me?"

Harlow always asked me things like this. She didn't ignore me the way my other clients did, and she didn't look down her nose when she spoke to me. Instead, she acted like I was her partner. She appreciated my help, even though she was paying me to do it.

"I would like that, and thanks for asking, but I have to meet someone tonight. I need to finish up and get home to clean up before I go," I wished I didn't have to decline the offer. I had skipped breakfast and was hungry.

Harlow beamed at me. "Well, I can fix that. You have milk and cookies with me, and I'll give you a lift home. You'll be back much sooner with a ride. And don't tell me no. You turned me down last week, and my brother called to make sure I gave you a ride. I explained that you wouldn't let me, and he blamed me. So from now on, I'm driving you. No arguments." She turned and hurried after Lila Kate, who was now crying louder since she'd heard Harlow's voice.

It took me a moment to steady myself. I pressed my hands to my warm cheeks and wished I hadn't blushed. Mase had called to see if she was driving me home. He was thinking about me aside from when I called him. The crazy grin that was stuck to my face every time I thought of Mase was back.

When I had started dusting the steps again, Harlow reappeared at the top of them holding a wide-eyed, smiling Lila Kate. She was happy now that she had her mommy. The little girl could light up a room.

"Lila Kate is expecting you for cookies and milk, too. So you can't turn her down. No one is allowed to tell her no. Just ask her daddy," Harlow said, starting down the steps. "Let's go enjoy our break,"

I wasn't going to argue. It would be rude, and, well, if Mase wanted her to give me a lift so badly that he was calling to bug her, I wasn't telling her no. Besides, I really was hungry.

The Carters' kitchen reminded me of something from a sitcom. It was warm and lived-in, but no expense had been spared. Harlow placed Lila Kate in her swing, which sat looking out the bay window into the backyard. "You swing and watch the birds, and I'll get your bottle ready," she told her daughter, as if the baby understood what she was saying. Then she turned to me. "I can make you coffee if you prefer it. I can't drink coffee unless it's decaf, and then I can only have a little. But I do have it here. Grant drinks it."

Milk sounded just fine to me. "I like milk," I replied. "Can I help you?"

"Just sit down and take a breather. You've been working for hours nonstop. You should take lunch breaks."

I wasn't supposed to take breaks longer than fifteen minutes every two hours with the agency. And I had found out that most of the people I cleaned for didn't like to see me take a break. If they were home, then they wanted me to work until I was done. So I did.

The Carters' house was different in many ways. That was one of them. It was also my favorite because I got to watch a happy, normal family. It wasn't something I had seen before. The way Harlow adored her daughter made me smile, but there was always a pang in my chest for what I didn't have. For what my mother chose never to give me. Love.

Grant Carter was breathtaking when he held his daughter. Or even when he saw her from across a room. His entire face was full of love and complete devotion. There was no question in anyone's mind that he would protect his little girl at all costs. I had caught myself wondering more than once if my real father would have been that way. Did he even know about me?

I shook off the thought again and focused on the Carters. I wouldn't think about my family or my past. It would only lead me to a depressed state. I worked hard not to spend time dwelling on those things.

This house was a home. It was a happy, safe place. Even though it was one of the smaller houses I cleaned, it was still the one I looked forward to every week.

Harlow placed a glass of milk and a plate with two big chocolate chip cookies in front of me. "Here you go," she said, and placed the same thing in front of the seat across from me. "I'll try to sneak a little before Lila Kate remembers it's time to eat. Her bottle will be ready in a few minutes anyway. It needs to warm up." She sat down.

"These smell delicious," I told her, hoping that was a good excuse for devouring them. I was even hungrier than I'd thought, and the smell was going to make it hard to take little, delicate bites.

"They should be. It's my grandmother's recipe. She made the best cookies," Harlow replied. "Grant loves them."

As I'd predicted, I ended up eating the first one in three bites. Harlow was grinning as she watched me. She was also chewing away happily, so that made it less embarrassing. But these cookies were seriously yummy.

"Have you spoken with my brother since he went back to Texas?" Harlow asked, surprising me.

I nodded, wondering if I should give her more information. Did Mase want her knowing that he and I were talking? She might think it was about something else and get the wrong idea. I felt comfortable with Harlow, but telling her that I had dyslexia was another thing. How would I explain how I had made it this far not being able to read and write without getting into the other details of my past?

"He seems . . . concerned about you. Mase is the protective sort, but I can't remember him being quite so concerned about someone who wasn't family. Until you." A smile tugged at the corners of her lips.

Oh, no. She was getting the wrong idea. If I didn't explain this to her, she would say something to Mase, and I didn't want that. He had been so helpful, and I owed him this. Besides, it wasn't something to be ashamed of. Astor had told me that several times. He'd even had me repeat after him, "I am not less than. I have nothing to be ashamed of. I am a smart, capable person."

Remembering those words, I put the second cookie back on the little china plate. I met Harlow's curious gaze. "I call

Mase after my lessons with Dr. Munroe." I paused for a beat. "I . . . I have dyslexia, and until Mase found Dr. Munroe, I didn't know why I couldn't read and write. Words are so difficult for me. Your brother took the first step and found a specialist who pointed me in the right direction. He's just helping me because he's a good man."

Harlow's gaze stayed on me for several seconds, and I had to drop my eyes to the cookie waiting before me. I didn't want her to read what I couldn't hide on my face.

Mase

"It's a woman," Major said, as he opened my fridge and grabbed a beer. "I know the signs. You can try to shit me with whatever hogwash you wanna spew, but I've been there, dude."

Major was becoming a pain in my ass. He was my step-father's nephew, and I'd been raised with him as my cousin. Although we weren't related by blood, it didn't seem to matter. I had needed his help today with the horses, but I was ready for him to leave now. Reese would be calling soon. And Major was the last person I wanted here when she called.

"We're done for the day. Take the beer and go home. I'm getting a shower, then hitting the sack. I'm beat." I walked past the kitchen and toward my bedroom.

"Right there. That is. Bull. Shit," he called after me. "Woman bullshit. Seen it. Know it."

I hated how close he was to the truth. Reese was on my mind most of the day, every damn day. I looked forward to her calls way more than I should. But damn, her voice made me smile. Hearing how excited she was over her progress also got to me. "Leave," I fired back, and slammed the bedroom door behind me.

I had started pulling off my boots when my cousin decided

to bang on my door. "Who is it? Can't be Cordelia. You'd have done more than tap that ass years ago if you wanted her. She's more than available. Wait . . . Rosemary Beach. You met someone there, didn't you? Rich babe? Got cash? Got a sister? No, wait, I don't want her sister. I still want a go at *your* hot single sister."

God, could he be any more annoying? "Go on, Major. I'm not giving you anything. There is no woman. Leave and let me shower in peace. Fucking pest."

Major's laughter filtered through the door. "Thou doth protest too much." He slapped the door one more time. "Fine. Be like that. But you'll admit it soon enough. Or I'll figure this shit out."

I didn't respond to him. I waited until his footsteps had moved toward the front door. When the door opened and closed, I let out a sigh of relief. Glancing at the clock, I saw that I had forty-five minutes before she was due to call. I could shower and grab something to eat.

If Major knew about Reese, he'd say something to my mother. Then I'd never hear the end of it. I loved my mom, but she would ask questions. I wasn't ready to answer questions. I wasn't even sure where this was going with Reese. Denying that I was attracted to her was pointless. I had admitted that to myself.

Hell, I'd been thinking about the freckle under her ass since the first moment I saw her. But it was more than just lust now. I liked Reese. I liked the woman she was inside. At first, I'd been afraid it was pity and that my emotions were wrapped up in feeling sorry for her and wanting to help her.

I didn't think that anymore. Reese didn't want pity. She

didn't require it. She was tough. Much tougher than I had given her credit for. I respected her ability to roll with the punches of life and keep fighting. With a body like hers, she could have used those assets to follow another path in life. One where her looks paid the bills. But she hadn't done that. Instead, she worked hard cleaning houses, and she was proud of her job.

There was much more to Reese than I had first assumed. So much more than I could have expected. And she was getting to me, slowly reeling me in, and she didn't even realize it. But I had to face the fact that she might not want that. It was very likely that Reese wasn't interested in me for anything more than friendship.

Maybe that was for the best. For starters, we lived several states away from each other. That in itself was an issue. And it wasn't like she would up and move just to date me, and moving my ranch to Rosemary Beach was impossible. I had a job and a future here.

Stepping into the shower, I decided that I wouldn't think about that now. There was no point. This needed to be taken slowly. My fantasies about her would remain just that.

✖

Thirty minutes later, my phone rang as I was standing on my front porch finishing a beer, still thinking about her.

"Hey," I said, as I answered on the first ring.

"Hey. I'm earlier than usual. I hope that's OK." She sounded excited.

I smiled. "Yeah. That's fine. I wasn't doing anything but waiting for you to call anyway."

"Oh," was her only response.

"How did tonight go?" I asked. Astor Munroe was also giving me full reports once a week via e-mail. He had agreed not to mention the fact that I was paying him to help Reese. I didn't think she would be as willing to work with him if she knew. I wanted her mind completely free of any distractions from learning.

"Great. I read him a chapter of the book he had given me last week. It wasn't a picture book. It was my first chapter book. I wasn't fast or anything, but I read it without panicking or getting a word wrong. I also took a spelling test. The first one I've ever passed in my life," she added, sounding giddy. The idea of never being able to pass a spelling test sliced me a little inside. I hated thinking about the little girl who had struggled and been ignored.

"That's amazing. I'm so proud of you, but then, I knew you could do it. Never doubted you," I assured her. "I'm still waiting for you to be brave enough to read to me."

That always made her go silent on me. She was still scared to read to me, but dammit, I wanted her to trust me. I wanted her to feel comfortable with it. Knowing she read for Astor made me jealous of the man. Which was ridiculous but true.

I started to assure her that she didn't have to if she wasn't ready, but she spoke first.

"OK. Um, let me go get the book I read tonight," she said softly.

Maybe it was selfish to let her do this when she was obviously so nervous, but I wanted this bad. "I'm honored," I admitted.

A soft laugh came over the phone. "I keep telling myself

you've heard me sing, and my reading isn't as bad as *that*, so I can do this."

Only this woman could make me grin like a fool over the damn phone. "This is true," I agreed, teasingly.

She laughed again. "It's not a deep read or anything. Tell me when you've had enough. My feelings won't be hurt. This may bore you to death."

I'd let her read the whole book if she would. "I will. Read to me."

For the next thirty minutes, I settled into the rocking chair on my front porch with my legs propped on up the railing and listened to Reese's sweet voice reading to me over the phone. She only got hung up a few times, and I helped her quickly so she wouldn't get nervous and stop on me.

It was the best thirty minutes I'd had all week.

Reese

After my first time reading to Mase, our twice-a-week phone calls became a nightly thing. On the days when I didn't go to my lessons, Mase called me. He wanted me to read to him before he went to bed. I wondered how much he really wanted to hear me read. I had a feeling he was trying to get me to practice with him. This was his way of making sure that I got comfortable reading in front of people.

Hearing his voice at night before bed was comforting. It was odd how easily I drifted off to sleep once I had talked to him. He always ended the calls with "Good night and sweet dreams." As if my body was at his command, I had exactly that. Each night was good, and my dreams were always of him. So they were very sweet.

Getting control over my growing affection for this man was something I needed to do, and fast. Mase was a friend. One of the best a girl could have. I didn't want to mess that up for anything. And if I made him uncomfortable, this could all end. That was too depressing to consider.

"Earth to Reese. I'm asking you a question. Where did you go?" Jimmy sat down across from me on the sofa.

His visit was unexpected, but he'd come with ice cream

again, and I couldn't kick him out. But my phone would ring soon, and I wanted Jimmy to be gone when that happened. I didn't want to tell Mase that I couldn't talk.

"Sorry. I was thinking about stuff. Ignore me. I'm tired."

Jimmy cocked an eyebrow as if he didn't believe me. "Really? Too tired for rocky road?"

No. I wasn't too tired for rocky road. I was too excited about hearing Mase's voice for rocky road. "Of course not." I took the spoon he'd stuck into the container for me and took a big bite.

"Easy, girl. Brain freeze is a bitch," Jimmy warned.

Smiling, I silently agreed and took my time before another bite.

"Next weekend. I'm not waiting anymore. You are going out with the doctor. It's a double date. You pick the night. Friday or Saturday. Because it is happening. I'm done waiting for you."

Crap. He wasn't letting this go. He mentioned it at least once a week. I had been avoiding answering.

But maybe this was a good thing. I was so focused on Mase, and that couldn't be good. If I dated, I might be able to distract myself. That seemed highly unlikely, but at least if Mase was getting the idea that I was interested in him, this would throw him off. He wouldn't have to worry about my affection for him. And that meant he wouldn't stop calling me.

"Friday night would be best."

Jimmy beamed and punched a fist into the air. "Yes! Victory! Score!"

Before I could respond, my phone rang, and I glanced down at my lap to see the cowboy boots on my screen. I picked it up before Jimmy saw it. "This is important. It's about a class I'm thinking of taking. Can we finish this tomorrow, maybe?"

He looked curious, but I knew the pleading look I was giving him would be enough to get him to leave. The phone stopped ringing but immediately rang again, and I answered it before it stopped. "Hey, give me just a minute," I told Mase, then stood up to open the door for Jimmy, who was watching me with even more open curiosity now.

"I don't believe you, but I'll let it slide," Jimmy whispered, wagging a finger at me.

I closed the door and breathed a sigh of relief. "Sorry. Jimmy was here. He's gone now," I explained.

"Did I interrupt anything?"

"Only rocky road ice cream and a nosy friend."

He chuckled. "You could have told me you were enjoying some ice cream with him. I'd have called back later."

Oh, no, I couldn't. Not when my day revolved around these phone calls from him. "That's OK. We were finished," I lied.

The sound of tires squealing rattled the apartment, and before I could figure out what was going on outside, a gunshot rang out. I froze. I couldn't move. Surely that wasn't what I had heard. Maybe the car backfired. This was a safe area; it was why I had chosen this apartment.

A series of shots rang out, and I fell to my knees behind the chair in front of me. Screams echoed in the streets, and for the first time, I regretted being on the first floor. I felt completely open and vulnerable, unable to get to safety.

"Reese, are you OK?" Mase shouted over the phone. I realized he'd been asking over and over, but I was too shocked for his voice to register.

My hand was covering my mouth, and I wondered if I had screamed. My eyes were glued to the window, while the screaming outside continued. Someone needed to call the cops. Me. I needed to. *Oh, God.*

"I need to call the police. There are gunshots outside and screaming. I have to call and get help," I told him, not wanting to hang up. I was terrified, and knowing that Mase was on the phone gave me some comfort. Even though he could do nothing.

"Fuck! Get on the ground. Lie flat behind your sofa. Don't move or answer the door. Call the cops *now*. Then call me back," Mase ordered, then ended the call.

My hands were shaking as another gunshot sounded. Voices were yelling unintelligible words along with the screaming. I crawled over to the sofa and lay flat behind it, then tried to call 911 as the panic set in. The numbers on my phone began to shift and blur. Tears of frustration filled my eyes.

My body jerked as I sobbed, trying to figure out where the 9 was, but then the police sirens joined the noise outside, and blue lights flashed through my window. I dropped my phone onto the carpet and covered my face with my hands.

Taking deep breaths to calm down, I listened as more sirens joined the scene, followed by an ambulance. But I didn't move. Not once.

I lay there as the screaming stopped, but there was still yelling, and people were crying. I was afraid to move, even though I knew the police were outside now.

A knock sounded on my door, and I froze. "Police," a loud voice called out.

Police. At my door. *Oh, God.* I had to get up. My legs were shaking horribly, and my heart was still racing.

The knock came again. "Police!" he called out again.

I grabbed the doorknob and looked through the peephole. There was indeed an officer at my door. His determined scowl only terrified me more, if that was possible.

Opening the door, I stared at the man.

He flashed me his badge. "Officer Milton, ma'am. I need to ask you a few questions."

Me? Why me? I nodded and forced myself to take a breath.

"Did you see anything?" he asked, standing there as the lights flashed and the sirens whined behind him. Someone was covered with a plastic sheet. Bile rose up my throat, and I squeezed the doorknob to keep from falling when my knees went weak.

"Oh, God," I managed to whisper.

"Do you know Melanie and Jacob Sanders? They live three doors down from you."

I shook my head no. I didn't know anyone who lived around me. Except Jimmy. I had kept myself closed off from everyone else. But three doors down, there was a married couple. I had met the husband, unfortunately. He had given me the creeps. I had been walking to the car one day, and he'd whistled and called my ass "luscious."

"I don't know them. I only know Jimmy . . . Jimmy Morrison. He lives in apartment two D. He was just here before . . . Oh, God! Jimmy was just here. He had to walk to the stairs to get back to his apartment. It happened right after he left."

The cop's expression softened. "Jimmy Morrison is fine. He's the one who called in the disturbance. He saw most of it happen and is currently giving his statement. He knew the victim."

My phone was ringing. Mase was calling me back.

"If you remember anything, please call the office. Jimmy will have confirmed that he'd just left your apartment. If he doesn't, we will be back to talk to you. I do need your name, for the record."

"Reese Ellis," I replied, as my phone stopped ringing and started back up again.

"Thank you, Miss Ellis."

I nodded and closed the door as the cop walked to the next door. I bolted it before answering my phone. "The cops were here," I told Mase. "They asked me a few questions."

"You're OK." He let out a sigh of relief.

"Yes. Jimmy saw it. He's with the police now, giving his statement. I'm not totally sure what happened; the police didn't even tell me who the victim was, but a married couple a few doors down were involved somehow. All I did was hear the shots and the screams. Nothing more. But Jimmy was out there. He could have been shot."

"But he wasn't. Don't think about that," Mase said in a firm voice.

I nodded, even though he couldn't see me. He was right. I didn't need to dwell on something that didn't happen.

"Did you lock your door?" he asked.

"Yes, it's bolted."

"When Jimmy is done with the cops, he'll come tell you what happened. Just sit down and relax. I'll talk to you until then. You're going to be fine. I know you're upset and scared."

Just hearing his voice calmed me. I sat down on the sofa and watched the lights continue to flash outside.

"Read to me, Reese. It will take your mind off this."

I wasn't sure I could. My vision had totally blurred when I was upset earlier. Focusing didn't work when you were panicking. "I don't know if I can," I admitted.

"Just try," he said gently.

Because I wanted to please him. I tried.

Mase

Listening to her soft voice was the only thing that could calm me down. I was standing on my front porch with my boots on and my keys in my hand. When she hadn't called me back and wouldn't answer her phone, I'd been ready to go after her.

If she hadn't answered that last ring, I was going to call Grant and Rush to check on her, and then I was going to ask my father to order a private jet immediately and fly my ass to Rosemary Beach. Hell, my knees had almost buckled with relief when she'd finally answered the phone. I wanted Jimmy to get his ass to her and tell her what happened so she would know. And so she wouldn't be alone.

But until then, I wasn't letting her go. Fuck, I wouldn't let her go once Jimmy got there. I was seriously close to calling Rush and Grant to stay with her until I could get there.

She was struggling more tonight than she had in weeks as she read to me. I hated the thought of her being scared and alone. I also hated the fact that she lived in that apartment by herself. It wasn't safe. This proved that.

"Jimmy's at the door," she said.

"I want to hear what he has to say," I told her. I didn't want her hanging up on me.

"OK. I'll just, um, set the phone down."

I waited as she opened the door. Jimmy asked her if she was OK, and it sounded like he was hugging her. She let out a small sob and asked him if he was OK. Then he was assuring her that he was fine.

"What happened?" Reese asked him.

"I don't know the full story. When I was headed to the stairs, I heard wheels screech, and then I heard Jacob screaming at Melanie that she was a slut. Melanie began calling him names, too, and then he just pulled out a gun from his waistband and shot at her. She took off running and screaming, and I was trying frantically to dial nine-one-one when the second round went off. I saw . . ." Jimmy paused. "I need to sit down. Shit, I'm gonna need a stiff drink tonight."

"You don't need to be alone," Reese told him.

"My man is on his way. He'll hold me tonight," Jimmy replied.

"Good."

That didn't help me. I didn't like the idea of Reese being alone tonight, either. I also fucking hated that she was on the first floor. It was dangerous down there.

"I saw her go down. She just crumpled to the ground. There was a pool of blood around her, and she wasn't moving. It wasn't the smart thing to do, but I went running toward her. And then the bastard fired at me. He missed and took off, but I don't know if I'll ever be able to get that image out of my head of a gun pointed at me."

Shit.

"Oh, no, Jimmy!"

"The guy in her apartment that she'd been having an affair with took off running in his underwear like a punk-ass. The cops caught him, though. He didn't get far. He was scared shitless. They got Jacob, too. He stuck around too long, then ran his car into a ditch going too fast around a curve. The cops got him as he was running away from the car. This place was a fucking circus. People opening their doors and screaming and yelling. No one was trying to help; they were just panicking. He just . . . killed her. Shot her dead. Damn psycho. They'd been married for three years."

"That's awful." Reese's voice was off. She was upset. And he was going to fucking leave her alone by herself while he cuddled up with his boyfriend?

"I've got to go get a shower and some tequila. Anything to wash this shit out of my head. You stay bolted up. You'll be safe, though. The cops will be all over this scene most of the night. It's fine. But if you need me, just call."

I heard Reese stand up and follow him to the door. "I'm glad you're OK," she said, and her voice cracked.

"Ah, girl. I'm fine," he assured her. "Just fucked-up in the head after watching that. I wasn't close to Melanie. Hardly knew her, but damn, it doesn't matter. Seeing a person die is tragic. So fucking tragic."

They said their good-byes, and I could hear Reese locking the door as the bolt slid into place.

"Hey. Did you hear everything?" she asked me. There was a tightness in her voice. Like she was trying not to cry.

"Yeah. That's messed up. But it wasn't a random act of violence. So no one is coming back to fire any more shots. You're safe," I assured her.

She didn't reply right away. I wondered if she was afraid to sleep now. After all that, she needed someone to be there with her and hold her.

"Go get ready for bed. Lay the phone down. I'll wait. Then take me to bed with you. I'll be right here at your ear. We can talk until you fall asleep. OK?"

"OK . . . you don't mind doing that?"

I wasn't going to be able to sleep tonight. I'd be worried about her. But she didn't need to know that. "I want to. Now, go get ready for bed. I'll wait."

"Thank you," she whispered.

While she got ready I put the phone on speaker and slipped it into my pocket, then headed inside. I put my beer can into the recycling bucket and washed up a few items in my sink.

Once I had that done, I went to my room. I brushed my teeth and stripped off the clothes I'd thrown on when I had been terrified for Reese and ready to go after her. Then I crawled into bed. Within minutes, her voice came back on the line.

"I'm back," she said, and I could hear the covers rustling.

I put one hand behind my head and lay on my back, staring at the ceiling fan in my room. Images of Reese in her bed were affecting me. I should have felt really damn guilty about it, but I couldn't help it.

"You want to read to me some more?" I asked, trying to think of anything to say to get my mind off what she was wearing.

"No . . . not really. My brain is too tired to read," she said. She was moving around again. I could hear the muffled sounds of her sheets.

"What do you wear to sleep?" I asked her, before I could stop myself. I had to know. It was driving me crazy.

She let out a little laugh. "Nothing special. Just cutoff sweatpants and a tank top. It's soft and old, and I love to sleep in it."

I really wanted to see that soft, old tank top on her. The image in my head was wreaking havoc with my dick. It had stirred to life. But I had asked her what she was wearing, so I had brought this on myself. "What color is it?" I asked, wincing at my words. Dammit, what was I doing?

"Pink . . . or it was. It's faded now. Not so pink anymore," she replied hesitantly.

"Sounds comfortable."

"Mmm-hmm," was her only response. I started to change the subject for my own sake, but I didn't get a chance. "Do you just sleep in your underwear?" she asked, so softly I almost missed her question.

I thought she'd known just how naked I slept after I'd come out into the hall wrapped in a sheet the first time we met. "No," I replied, surprised that she'd asked me.

"Oh. I just assumed that since you came running into the game room in your boxers when I cut my hand, you must sleep in them."

A grin tugged at my lips. I'd snatched those out of my duffel and jerked them on while running down the hall toward her that morning.

"I put those on before coming to check on you," I explained.

A quick intake of breath was her only response.

"Sleeping naked ain't so bad. You should try it sometime," I teased, trying to lighten the mood, since she seemed at a loss for words.

Then she giggled. Mission accomplished. "I'm not sure I could do that," she said in an amused tone.

I was sure she could. My mind was playing with images of her doing just that. Then I joined her in my imagination, and it got even more interesting. Those long legs and that little freckle tucked below her ass would be the first things I explored. An image of her on my bed, with her ass stuck up in the air so I could nuzzle and kiss that freckle, sent a hard throb to my cock.

I wrapped my hand around it and squeezed, trying to calm it the fuck down. It was hot to the touch and wasn't going to cool itself anytime soon. Especially with Reese's voice heating me up.

"Reese, give me just a minute. I'll be right back," I told her.

"Oh, OK," she replied.

I hated that I was this fucking weak, but I had to get control of myself now if I was going to keep her on the phone until she went to sleep. I had to either jump into a cold shower or finish this fantasy in the privacy of my bathroom. I was in a hurry, and the image of Reese in my bed with her juicy round ass in the air was teasing me.

I closed the bathroom door, walked over to the wall, and leaned against it, then took my throbbing dick in my hand again. Slowly, I stroked it, as I licked Reese's ass and freckle, then shoved her legs apart and felt her hot pussy slick to my touch. My other hand would caress her ass, then slide up until it felt the hard nipples and heaviness of her breasts hanging down toward the mattress.

She would cry out as I slipped my tongue over her tender flesh, and her breasts would sway and bounce in my hand.

Fuck, that was all it took. I cried out as my release pumped out of me and covered my hand, still fisted tightly around it.

Since meeting Reese, I had been doing this more and more. I had tried a few cold showers, but I fucking hated them. This was the easier solution. And the less painful one. Plus, my fantasies about Reese were getting better and better.

Reese

Jimmy came by the next morning to tell me he had called in sick for the rest of the week and was going on a mini-vacation to get away from everything. He hadn't slept last night, and he was weepy today. His main concern had been me getting to work. Although I had assured him that I could walk, he said he wouldn't be able to relax and get his mind off everything if he was worried about me walking. So he had a guy he trusted come pick me up and take me home on the days I worked. He assured me that he'd known this guy forever, and he was a close friend of Mr. Kerrington. I had to promise him that I would ride with his friend, Thad, before he would leave. Because I was worried about him, I said OK. But this wasn't something I wanted to do at all. I would have much rather taken a cab. But Jimmy refused to accept that.

So now I stood outside my apartment waiting for a "black BMW with shiny silver wheels you can't miss" to drive up. Jimmy had also said that Thad had long blond hair and looked like he belonged on a surfboard.

Yellow crime-scene tape surrounded the door and side-walk three doors down. I cringed at the thought of the horror that had happened. Jimmy had seen it all. I worried about him, too. How could he get that out of his head and move on?

Last night, I had drifted off to sleep while Mase had put me on hold. It surprised me, really. Just knowing that he was there and wasn't leaving me had been enough to relax me. Then there had been the strange conversation we'd had about what we were sleeping in. He slept naked. The image of that man naked excited me. Which was going to be awkward when I had to see his face again.

The slick black BMW was hard to miss as it pulled into the parking lot. Even without seeing the wheels or the blond guy in the driver's seat, I knew it was him. No one in this apartment complex drove a car like that. I pulled my backpack up onto my shoulder and took a deep breath. Jimmy wouldn't send someone to get me who was dangerous. I could do this. I could.

The driver's-side door opened, and a tall guy with blond hair that curled just below his ears smiled at me. He had dark sunglasses on, so I couldn't see his eyes. However, he seemed safe. His smile was friendly, and again, Jimmy trusted him.

"Are you Reese?" he asked.

I nodded and stepped off the sidewalk and toward his car.

"Only Jimmy," Thad said, shaking his head and chuckling.

I didn't ask him what that meant. "Thanks for driving me. I'll pay for your gas," I told him as I got into the car.

Thad frowned. "Uh, no, you won't. I can give a beautiful girl a ride to work and back."

I didn't tense when he called me beautiful. That was a positive sign. I was progressing. Not all men were bad. Jimmy, Mase, and Dr. Munroe had taught me that. Then there was the way Grant Carter adored his wife and child. My thoughts about men were changing. The longer I stayed in Rosemary Beach, the more I saw the good side of humanity.

"Did Jimmy tell you to take me to the Kerrington Club? I can walk to work from there." Lately, Jimmy had been taking me to the houses I worked at instead of letting me walk. It was something I knew Mase had mentioned to him.

"I was told you needed to be taken to Nan's today. I hear she's coming back in the next two weeks. Oh, joy," Thad said, looking at me like I understood what he was talking about.

I had never met Nan, but from what everyone, including her brother, said about her, I wasn't sure I wanted to. I liked cleaning her house. I needed that job. But she was beginning to terrify me. I would have to tell her about the mirror when she returned. I dreaded that. "I don't think I'm looking forward to meeting her," I admitted to Thad. "No one seems to like her very much."

Thad let out a bark of laughter. "Understatement of the year."

Oh, wow. I wished she could just stay in Paris.

"You heard those shots last night?" Thad asked, changing the subject. "Seeing the crime-scene tape is freaky shit."

I nodded and pushed the memory of last night out of my head. "Yeah," was my only response. Then I focused my attention out the window. I didn't want to talk about the shooting.

"Sorry. If she was your friend or something. I didn't mean to be disrespectful."

I continued looking out the window. "I didn't know her," I told him.

He was quiet then. I should probably have spoken up and not made it so awkward, but I wasn't sure what to say.

When he pulled up to Nan's gate and followed the curve of her driveway, I was relieved. I was looking forward to cleaning and enjoying my quiet time alone.

"I'll pick you up here around three."

"Yes, thank you." As weird as it was taking a ride from a stranger, it was nice to get to work faster.

Thad gave me a crooked grin. "No problem."

✠

That night, I told Mase about Jimmy leaving and Thad giving me a ride. He didn't seem thrilled by this, but I didn't ask him about it. We were friends, nothing more. Instead, I read two chapters to him. Just before we hung up, he asked me if I was in my pajamas yet.

"Yes," I replied, looking down at the cutoff sweats and tank top.

He sighed, then chuckled. "Sorry. I couldn't help myself. Good night, Reese."

"Good night, Mase."

"Sweet dreams."

He had no idea how sweet they would turn out to be.

Mase

My coffee was brewing, and I hadn't put on anything other than a pair of jeans, when a knock on my door disturbed my morning routine.

Annoyed, thinking it was Major here an hour early, I went and jerked open the door, ready to scowl at him. Instead, it was Cordelia.

She hadn't called or shown up since I had sent her home almost a month ago. I didn't step back and let her inside, because in the past, all our business had to do with sex, and I wasn't doing that anymore. Not when I was getting in deeper with Reese every day.

"I'm in love with you," she blurted out, as her eyes filled with tears.

Holy fuck, I did not need this today. Or any day. Cordelia was not ever supposed to fall in love with me. We'd had sex. That was it. Never any cuddling or kissing, just fucking.

Dammit.

"Cordelia, I'm sorry. But we went into that relationship knowing it was just a sex thing. I didn't know you had deeper feelings or were developing them. I would have put a halt to it a long time ago."

She sniffed, and her shoulders sagged in defeat. "So you really feel nothing? At all?"

Shit, I felt a fucking orgasm as I got my release. And yeah, her body had been nice and had felt good, and I'd enjoyed it, but that was it. Nothing emotional. I shook my head, hating to hurt her. "No. It was just sex for me. I thought that was all it was for you, too."

"Is there someone else?" she asked. "Is that why you're stopping with me?"

I wasn't sure how to answer this. Reese wasn't her business, but she was the reason this was ending. "I've got feelings for someone else, yes." There, I'd said it.

She covered her mouth on a sob. "You got into a relationship with someone else while you were fucking me?"

Shaking my head, I let out a frustrated groan. I just wanted some coffee. Not this. "I'm not in a relationship . . . yet," I told her. "But it doesn't matter. I want to be. I'm waiting for her."

Cordelia let out a hard laugh and wiped at the tears streaming down her face. "So the woman willing to give you everything isn't good enough. You want the one holding back, is that it? God, I hate men! You're all assholes!" Cordelia yelled the last bit. She pointed at me. "You will regret this. When you need me, you will regret this. All that hot sex we had was fantastic, and you know it. You will want my pussy and my ass again, and I won't give them to you. This is it, Mase. You've had your last chance."

I didn't have a response for that. I watched her turn and stalk back to her truck and climb inside. I closed the door and hoped she kept her word and that this was indeed it. I couldn't do this anymore and be nice about it. I hated hurting her, but she was pushing it.

My phone started ringing, and I looked longingly at the coffee in the pot. I really wanted that coffee. Frustrated, I reached for my phone. Why didn't everyone leave me alone? Dammit, I wanted a quiet morning.

Harlow's name lit up the screen.

"You OK?" I asked, anxious that something was wrong. She never called this early.

"I figured you'd be up already. Grant just told me something before he left for work that he heard yesterday that I thought was interesting news. I wanted to share it with you."

I was almost afraid to listen. She was up to something. I could hear it in her voice. Whatever information she had, she was enjoying it a little too much. "It's seven in the morning, Harlow. I've just gotten up, and I need coffee," I grumbled as I went to pour myself a cup.

"Drink your coffee, grumpy. I can tell you all the information I have while you drink it."

"Yeah," I agreed, only half listening to her. I was more focused on the hot liquid in the mug in front of me.

"Thad—you know, Woods Kerrington's friend—has been giving Reese a ride to and from work all week."

This was her news? Rolling my eyes, I walked outside to enjoy my coffee. "Already know that," I informed her.

"Oh. Well, do you know that he asked her out yesterday for this weekend, and she said yes?"

My hand paused in midair, the mug poised before my lips. *What the fuck?* "Reese is going on a *date* with *Thad*?" I asked, as I lowered my mug, still not sure that was what I had just heard. Reese was nervous with men. Thad was a player. I'd seen the dude in action. He was exactly the kind of guy I knew Reese didn't like to be around. *How the hell?* "Who told Grant this?" I asked, waiting for the punch line. This had to be a fucking joke.

"Thad. He asked her when he took her to work yesterday morning, and she said yes. Grant said he looked like a little boy who'd been given a shiny new toy. He wanted me to talk to Reese about Thad. He's kind of a man-whore, you know, and Grant doesn't want him to hurt Reese. But I figured I'd call you. Since you're friends with her, maybe you could call her and give her a heads-up."

She was so full of it. She knew this would piss me off. Harlow knew me too well. Like hell was Reese going out with Thad. If she wanted to date, then by God, she was gonna date me. "Thanks. I need to go. I'll talk to you later."

"OK, well, you will talk to her, right?"

I almost laughed at her fake concern. She knew good and well that I wasn't about to let that date happen. "I'll talk to her," I said, before hanging up the phone.

I slung back the coffee and let it burn my throat. I had to make a call to get a flight and then call Major to get him to take over everything I was abandoning to make sure Thad kept his playboy hands off what was mine.

Reese

Why had I said yes to Thad? Sure, he made me laugh, and he was nice, but I didn't want to go out with him. I wasn't sure how to say no, either. I didn't want to be rude. He had been so helpful all week, and after the first awkward day, we seemed to fall into an easy pattern.

Luckily, I didn't need to work today, so I didn't have to face him. But I would have to tomorrow night when he showed up for our date. It had been on the tip of my tongue to tell Mase last night, but something had held me back. Just because I had a crush on Mase, that didn't mean the feelings were mutual. Even if he liked to know when I was in my pajamas, that didn't mean he wanted to see me in them.

The idea made my cheeks hot.

Stop it, I scolded myself. I had to think about what I'd agreed to with Thad. A date. A real date. With a rich, attractive guy. Oh, no. What had I done? I couldn't do this.

Jimmy had been planning on me going on a double date with him tonight until the shooting. Then he'd left, and now he wasn't coming back until Sunday. I had talked to him two nights ago. When I realized he wouldn't be back for the double date, I had been relieved to get out of it. Then this had happened.

Mase would call me tonight. Should I mention it? Probably not. He didn't tell me when he had dates. Did he date? What if he'd been on dates lately? If he was dating, he got home early, because we talked at least by ten every night.

I looked down at my tank top and cutoff sweats and sighed. They really were worn out, but they were soft and comfortable. Women in Mase's world wore expensive silk and lace. I didn't own anything remotely sexy to sleep in. Until Mase, I hadn't desired anything like that. He had changed a lot of things. Maybe he was even the reason I'd said yes to Thad.

A loud, sharp knock on my door startled me, and I put my phone down on the sofa and stood up to see who was outside. I wasn't expecting anyone, and I really hoped that Thad wasn't coming for a visit. Not when I planned on talking to Mase on the phone tonight.

I peered through the peephole and gasped.

As if I had dreamed him up, there he stood outside my door. His face looked determined, and his hair was pulled back so that I could see the hard set of his jaw. He was here. Shock was replaced by concern as I unlatched and unbolted the door and swung it open.

"Mase, is everything OK?" I asked.

He stared at me. He began moving toward me, but then he stopped. "No. Can I come in?" he asked tightly.

I nodded and stepped back to let him inside. "What's wrong?" I asked, afraid to hear the answer. I was nervous.

Mase walked inside, and his gaze slowly trailed down my body, then back up again. Ever so slowly. When he made it back up to my face, there was a gleam there that made me shiver.

"That looks even better than I imagined. And trust me, baby, I've imagined you in that outfit a lot."

His voice sounded like he was caressing the words instead of saying them. The dark tone in his voice made me shiver again. I couldn't speak. Not now. He had taken all my words with those looks.

"I don't want you going out with Thad," he said firmly, snapping me out of my strange haze. His jaw was clenched tightly again, and that strange gleam in his eyes had returned.

"How did you know?" I asked him. *And why do you care?* I thought silently.

"He told Grant," he replied. That was answer enough. "I was giving you time. You seemed skittish. I didn't want to push you. But if you're going on a date with someone, it's gonna be me, Reese. Not fucking playboy Thad."

He said the last part in a growl that caused me to jump.

"He doesn't know the first thing about you. He won't know how to read your expressions to know when you like something or not. He won't know when he's making you uncomfortable or when you need help reading something. He won't know that you have two different laughs. One is real, and the other means you're nervous. He won't know shit. But I do."

Was Mase Manning really trying to persuade me to go out with him? Did he think he had to give me a sales pitch so I would buy in?

"And he'll make a mistake. He will do something to hurt you, and I'll kill him. I'm not a violent guy, but fuck me, if he were to hurt you, I'd lose it, baby. Lose my mind. So the way I see it, you need to cancel that date with him and make new plans. With me."

Before he could start trying to convince me again, I smiled. "OK."

He opened his mouth, then closed it. His eyes flashed something that could only be labeled pleasure, and he took a step toward me. "OK?" he asked.

I nodded. "Yes. OK," I repeated.

A grin tugged up one corner of his beautiful mouth. "OK as in you're gonna cancel that date with Thad and make new plans with me? All weekend?"

All weekend. He was here for the whole weekend? I nodded, unable to keep from smiling even more brightly. I was going to get to spend the whole weekend with Mase. He had come here to see me.

Me!

Mase closed the distance between us, and his hands reached up and cupped my face. My body tensed but then eased almost immediately. His smell met my nose, and I was comforted.

"I'm going to kiss you now, Reese. Can't hold back any longer," he said, his breath a whisper over my lips before the soft plumpness of his mouth touched mine.

He was so gentle as he pressed soft kisses at each corner of my mouth before the tip of his tongue slid along my bottom lip, as if asking me to open. I had seen people kiss. I knew you opened your mouth, but it seemed so intimate. I wasn't sure if I was ready for that. Or if I would be any good at it.

"Please open for me," he begged against my lips, and I realized I would probably do anything if he asked me to.

I opened my mouth—and gasped when his tongue slid inside and brushed against my tongue, as if in a dare to play. He tasted like peppermint. A low moan came from his chest, and one of his hands went to my lower back and pressed me closer to him as he slid his other hand into my hair and cupped the back of my head. The way he held me was different. He was careful with me.

His tongue continued to tease mine, so I ran my tongue over his and began exploring the minty taste of his mouth. When my tongue ran over his bottom lip, his hand against my lower back fisted. With a sharp intake of breath, his body trembled.

So I did it again.

This time, he made a pleased sound in his throat, then broke the kiss and rested his forehead against mine. "I knew you'd be sweet. But damn, baby, you taste like my own little heaven."

My chest swelled, and I smiled. I hadn't done anything wrong. He enjoyed it as much as I did. "Can we do it again?" I asked him, resting my hands on his biceps.

A low chuckle vibrated in his chest. "Yeah. We can kiss all you want to."

His lips brushed mine again before pressing closer and opening back up. I savored the feel of touching him in such a personal way. His hands rested on my waist, and whenever I licked the roof of his mouth or tasted his lips, his hands tightened only briefly.

My body was tingling all over, and I wanted to crawl into his lap and do this all night. I was enjoying myself, and I was amazed that I was enjoying myself so much. My breasts ached, and my body instinctively pressed closer to his to find relief.

The second my chest pressed against him, he pushed me several inches away. Kissing over.

Mase was watching me as if he wasn't sure how to handle me. He was keeping me at arm's length. Literally.

"I need to know what I can and can't touch," he said, sounding out of breath. "I know something makes you cautious and nervous. I've watched you closely, and I read body language well. But you're confusing me, Reese."

Without asking me to tell him about my past, he was letting me know that he knew something was there. Something haunted me. And he was being careful not to scare me. The little bit of my heart that I thought I still had possession of fled. Mase Manning now had it all.

"I liked what we were doing," I told him, hoping that all the love I felt for this man wasn't shining on my face like the bright ray of sunlight that was warming up all the things inside me that had long felt cold.

Mase smirked, then shook his head. "Yeah, I got that you liked the kissing. But getting close and pressing those sweet . . ." He trailed off as his gaze flicked to my chest, and he let out a small groan before looking back up at my face. "My hands are going to want to explore. I've been fantasizing about your body for a while now. I need to know where my hands can and can't go."

He had been fantasizing about me? Oh, my.

Where could he go? My heart wanted him everywhere, but I knew my head might not agree. The problem was, I wasn't sure what would set me off. So far, what we were doing was nothing like the nightmare I'd lived through. It was wonderful. It helped hold back the ugly memories. I wanted more of this in hopes that it would drown out the past.

"What part of me do you want to touch?" I asked.

His eyes went back to my chest. "I'd like to start there," he said in a hoarse whisper.

My breasts began to tingle and ache at the nipples, like they knew they were getting attention from this beautiful man and liked it. They were as shameless as I was. I nodded, and his eyelids lowered as he kept his heated gaze locked on my now heaving chest. I was having a hard time breathing, because I was that excited to feel Mase's hands on me.

He took a step toward me, and his hooded gaze met mine again. I think I stopped breathing in that moment when his hand lifted, and I felt the warmth from his skin as he cupped his palm around my needy breast.

I inhaled sharply, and he studied me carefully. He didn't move until I began breathing again normally. Or as normally as can be expected when your breast is being fondled by the man you're in love with. His thumb grazed over my nipple, and I grabbed his biceps to steady myself. His eyes were locked on my chest now. With the pad of his thumb, he circled and teased my nipple, causing me to make some sounds I had never made before.

When his other hand moved toward me, I had to close my eyes and take a deep breath for fear of passing out. Just as he'd done with the other breast, he gently cupped it, then began paying close attention to the nipple. I suddenly hated the tank top I loved to sleep in. It was in the way. But the idea of Mase taking the tank top off me and actually looking at my bare breasts was as terrifying as it was exciting.

"Is this OK?" he whispered almost reverently.

"Yes," I replied.

"I want to kiss you again while I touch you," he said, studying my lips. "Can we lie down on your bed?"

My bed. That was more. A lot more.

But I had Mase in my bed every night. Even if it was just on the phone.

"Yes," I told him, before I could freak out and change my mind.

His left hand slid down my stomach and hip, and then he took my hand in his. He didn't say anything else as he led me over to the bedroom door. The lamp beside the bed was the only light in the room.

His hand left mine, and he sat down on the edge of the bed. I watched, fascinated, as he tugged off his boots and placed them on the floor, his gaze never leaving me.

"Come here," he said, with a crook of his long finger.

At this point, the man could tell me to go jump off a bridge, and I was pretty sure I'd ask him which one.

He took both my hands and pulled me into his lap.

I had to straddle him with my knees on the bed. He tilted his mouth to fit across mine, and then all thought of nerves vanished as he kissed me again. The wonders he could accomplish with the slip of his tongue. I wrapped my arms around his neck and sank into him . . . until the hardness I remembered from my past was pressing against me. Then I froze.

Without warning, the memories came back, taunting me. I shuddered and jumped off him and backed away, afraid that he'd see the horror in my eyes. That he'd know exactly how dirty I was. I didn't want to make him dirty. What had I been thinking? I couldn't do this. Mase was so good and nice and kind. He didn't know me. He thought he did. But he had no idea.

"Come back to me, Reese. Don't you go there," he said, his hands taking both of mine and holding me. "Look at me, baby."

Mase

The broken, terrified expression on her face made me physically ill. I never wanted to be the reason that darkness came over her. "Please, Reese, look at me. In my eyes. Focus on me. Nothing else," I encouraged her, as I held her hands firmly in mine while letting her maintain some space between us. My initial reaction had been to pull her tightly into my arms and hold her. But those eyes had stopped me.

She blinked her eyes several times, and her gaze cleared up as she did what I asked. She was back with me. The demons tormenting her were once again pushed away. "I'm sorry," she whispered, her voice thick with emotion.

"No. Never be sorry. Nothing is your fault. With me, you never have to apologize," I said.

Her shoulders sank in defeat, and she looked like she was on the verge of tears. I wasn't letting her do that. Not now. Not after she'd given me so much, entrusted me with so much.

"Can I just hold you? Nothing more. Just let me hold you." It was supposed to be a question, but it had turned into pleading.

She nodded and stepped toward me. I gathered her into my arms and wrapped them around her. Slowly, her arms slid around my waist, and she held on to me just as fiercely.

We didn't speak or move. We just stood there like that, holding each other for several minutes. I reassured myself that she was here and she was going to be OK. I would be there right beside her through all of this. Whatever it was.

I pressed a kiss to the top of her head, then pressed my cheek against the silky locks. The cinnamon sweet cream smell that I loved engulfed me, and I closed my eyes, wishing I could wipe away every bad thing that had happened to her.

"I hate him. I don't know who he is, but I loathe him with every fiber of my being," I whispered against her hair.

She tensed in my arms for a moment, and then her body relaxed as her arms tightened around me as if she was seeking safety and comfort from me. I could give her that. Even if she wasn't ready for me to give her other things, I could give her peace.

"It's late. You need to go to bed," I told her, wanting nothing more than to crawl into that bed with her. Even if it was just to sleep.

"Will . . . will you stay here tonight?" she asked against my chest.

"Nowhere else I'd rather be."

She pulled back from me, and I let her go. She walked over to the bed, pulled back the covers, and climbed under them. Then she patted the spot beside her. "Sleep here. Beside me."

Her wish was my command. I lay down beside her but stayed on top of the covers. I was fully clothed, so I didn't need covers anyway. Holding out my arm, I looked at her curled up on her side, watching me. "Come here," I said, and she immediately moved to tuck herself into the crook of my arm and shoulder. I wrapped my arm around her and held her.

Staring at the ceiling, I wondered how I would go back home on Sunday morning. Leaving her wasn't going to be easy. I didn't like thinking of her here alone.

The need to protect her had grown into something fierce and possessive inside of me. I thought of her all the time, and all I could think was that I wanted her safe. I wanted her with me. I didn't want anyone else touching her or comforting her. Just me.

I was supposed to fix her problems. I was the one who should be holding her when she cried. It drove me crazy to think of anyone else doing something for her that I should be doing.

This girl was making me crazy. I felt out of my depth with her. I didn't know why I had this insane urge to wrap her up and run off with her. It couldn't be healthy. I had always been protective of Harlow and my mother. But other than those two, no one else was that important to me.

Until now. And this was a league all its own.

Why her? Why was she affecting me like this? I had seen hot bodies before and gorgeous smiles. It was more than her outward appearance. Beautiful women only interested me for one thing. Reese had reached something else inside of me and squeezed it tight, from the moment I ran into the room and found her sitting on the floor surrounded by broken glass.

I had actually been pissed at the mirror for hurting her. Who gets fucking mad at an object?

"Mase?" her soft voice said against my chest.

The blood in my veins warmed and sped up with the sound of my name on her lips. Or at least, it felt like it. My whole body reacted to her. "Yes," I replied, gently wrapping a silky lock of her hair around my finger.

"It was my stepfather," she said, so softly I almost didn't hear her.

Everything in my chest felt like it was twisting into knots. It hurt to breathe. Holy fuck, it hurt so bad. I had to force oxygen into my lungs as the reality of what she had just admitted to me settled in. Rage unlike anything I'd ever experienced crashed through me, and I wanted to murder another human being for the first time in my life. No, I wanted to torture him slowly first. Listen to him scream in agony. Then I wanted to watch him die.

"Mase?" Reese's voice called my name again, and I inhaled sharply, putting the revenge and hate for a man I didn't know to the side. My girl needed me now. She didn't need me losing my shit over this. She'd trusted me with it.

"Yes, baby," I replied.

"I hate him, too."

Those four words just about undid me. "I'm going to wash it all away. I swear to God, I am, Reese. One day, all you will see or remember is me and what we feel like together. I swear."

She turned her head and kissed my chest, then snuggled closer to me. "I believe you."

Reese

It took me a few seconds to awaken fully and remember that I wasn't alone in my apartment. I didn't have to open my eyes to know that I was alone in bed. I could feel Mase's absence. His warmth was gone.

But he was in the other room. The smell of coffee filled the small apartment. And Mase's voice, although he was talking quietly, drifted through the closed door.

I made quick work of brushing my teeth and hair before going into the living room to face him after last night. The fact that he was here still amazed me. He had come to stop me from going on a date with Thad. And in return, I'd freaked out on him while doing something as simple as kissing and touching.

I opened the door and stepped into the room, and my eyes went straight to the tall form of perfection standing at the window with his back to me. He was on the phone. He was still wearing the jeans and T-shirt he'd had on last night, but his duffel bag sat on the sofa. He had come prepared.

"I'd rather not come, Harlow. I like Tripp and all, but I wasn't planning on being here this weekend, and I didn't come down for his party. I have other things I'd rather do tonight," he said in a frustrated tone, although he was still talking in a quiet voice.

His jaw worked as he listened to whatever his sister was saying. It seemed she really wanted him to go to a party tonight. I started to speak up and tell him he should go.

"Fine. I'll go if Reese wants to. But if she'd rather not, we're doing something else. End of discussion. Now, I love you, but I gotta go. I was going to try to make some breakfast before she wakes up."

I closed my mouth and stared in surprise at his back. He wanted to take me? To a party with his crowd? And he was going to make me breakfast? Not blurting out that I loved him was hard, because after listening to this conversation, I wanted to open the window and alert all the neighbors that I was in love with this man.

He turned, and his gaze locked on mine. A slow, sexy smile touched his lips, and I was sure I might swoon right here on the spot. "I gotta go. She's awake," he said into the phone, and ended his call.

I stood right where I was, unable to move, with that gleam in his eyes and the warmth of that gaze slowly trailing down my body and back up again.

"You even wake up gorgeous," he said in a gentle tone.

"Thank you," was my silly response. I didn't know what else to say.

"You hungry? I was going to take inventory and make us some breakfast," he said, as he walked over to the kitchen. "I've already made coffee."

"Yes, but I can make breakfast. I make really good homemade waffles." I followed him into the small kitchen area.

He glanced back at me over his shoulder. "Homemade waffles? Sold. All I can do is eggs and toast."

"Then you go sit over there, because both of us are not fitting into this kitchen."

He was pouring more coffee into his cup. Then he turned and walked back out of the corner hole I had for a kitchen. I may or may not have been checking out his butt in those jeans. I had to snap my head up when he turned back to me.

A knowing grin lit up his face, and he took a few steps back in my direction and placed his cup of coffee on the bar. "I'm going to admit something that I think you should know. I'm a bit of a caveman. The idea of you cooking for me turns me on." His voice dropped as he said the last part, then he bent his head and pressed a warm kiss to my lips.

I was ready for another round of kissing if he was. I went up on my tiptoes eagerly. I was five foot nine, but Mase was at least six-three or six-four. He made me feel short.

His hand slipped around to my lower back and pressed me closer to him, just before his mouth opened and I was given the yummy taste of his peppermint goodness. I moved my hands from his arms to his neck to help pull me up even farther on my toes.

Mase moved his hands over my butt and cupped it, and for a moment, we both stilled. When panic didn't set in, I leaned closer, and Mase inhaled sharply, then pulled me up his body while holding on to my bottom.

Just when I was getting ready to explore his lips some more, he broke the kiss and took a deep breath. "Reese, baby, I've got a thing for your ass. I've had a thing for your ass since day one. And now that I've got my hands on it, I need a minute to calm down without your hot little mouth turning me the fuck on," he said in a husky voice that made me shiver.

I ducked my head to hide my smile. He liked my butt. It was too fat, but he liked it. I couldn't keep from grinning.

"I see that smile," he said teasingly, as he squeezed my bottom in his hands and then groaned. "Fuck . . . that's nice," he said in my ear. "Either I carry you over to that sofa and continue to hold the finest ass in the world in my hands while I kiss you, or I let you go so you can make those waffles. Your choice. I want to do what you feel comfortable with."

This man and his words made me feel like goo inside. All melty and mushy. Who needs breakfast, anyway? "The sofa," I whispered, and he let out a pleased growl as he picked me up off the floor. I wrapped my legs around his waist, and he kept his hands on my bottom. In three long strides, we were sinking down onto the sofa. I felt the stiffness under my bottom, and he stilled.

I would not panic. This was Mase. This was Mase.

I kept my eyes locked on his handsome face and watched in fascination as his eyes flickered with something so sexy and needy that it made my center ache.

"You can pull your legs out and hold yourself up over my lap, if feeling what you do to me makes you nervous." His voice was tight, as if he was hurting somehow.

I moved so that my legs were folded on each side of his and I was straddling him. Just like last night. If I sank back down, I would feel his erection against me. But there was a tingling ache there that hadn't been there before. The idea of putting any pressure on it excited me.

Mase's hands flexed on my bottom, and he breathed out

heavily through his nose as we kept our gazes firmly locked on each other. Slowly, I let myself sink down onto his lap. The hard ridge of his penis fit right along the slit between my legs, and I gasped loudly when a spark that felt so good it was almost painful shot up my body from the contact between my legs.

Mase swallowed so hard I could hear him. His breathing was heavier now, and his hands had tightened their hold on my backside. "You OK?" he asked in a voice that sounded like he was in pain.

"Am I hurting you?" I asked, horrified. I hadn't even thought about how this might feel to him. I started to get up, and his hands immediately moved to my thighs as he held me down.

"No. No. Don't. This is . . . fuck, baby. I don't have words for what this is," he said, then let out a hard laugh as he laid his head back against the sofa and stared at the ceiling. "I need another minute."

His hands squeezed my thighs as he sat there like that. I admired the thickness of his throat. It even looked muscular. Did necks have muscles?

Feeling brave, I leaned forward and pressed a kiss to his neck. His hands flexed on my thighs, but that was the only move he made. So I kissed him again and inhaled his scent. He reminded me of leather and the outdoors. My body must have liked the two smells, because I had to press down to get some relief from the pulsing ache between my legs.

"Baby," he said softly.

"Yeah?" I asked, taking a small little taste of his skin with the tip of my tongue.

"Fuck," he groaned, and then I was moving away from him. His hands were on my waist, and he was placing me on the sofa as he got up and moved away as fast as he could.

I had been so lost in him I hadn't realized what was going on until I saw him stop and put his hands on his knees. I watched him take several deep breaths before he stood back up. I was afraid to ask him anything. I waited for him to say something first.

It seemed like forever before he finally turned around and looked at me. I had pulled my knees up in front of me and wrapped my arms around them. Something was wrong. I was waiting to hear him tell me what that was, exactly.

"I'm sorry. I . . . you're . . ." He stopped and laughed at himself, then shook his head in frustration. "I want you naked, Reese. I want my hands and mouth all over your sweet little body. I want to bend you over and kiss the freckle I know is right under your left butt cheek, the one I saw the first time I met you. I was greeted with your perfect ass bent over on display, and I've dreamed about that ass ever since. But more than that, I want you to always feel safe with me. I want to take it easy and slow with you, so I never have to see that haunted look in your eyes or the terror in your expression again. So we may have more moments when you press that"—he closed his eyes and breathed hard through his nose—"when you press against me and touch me in ways that drive me so crazy I'm afraid I will snap and touch you where you're not ready yet."

Hearing him tell me that he wanted to kiss me and touch me naked had my heart rate up again. It produced a mixture of fear and excitement. The sensation between my legs was still there. There was a needy ache that reminded me of a time when I was much younger and a guy I'd had a crush on at school cornered me and touched me, calling me beautiful.

After he'd ignored me and let his girlfriend call me horrible names the next day, that ache had never returned. Then other things happened that made any excitement in that part of my body die. Just remembering the past doused the feelings left behind from being in Mase's arms.

I was relieved that the ache was gone and sad that this kissing session with Mase was over when I stood up. "Then I guess it's time for breakfast," I said, forcing a smile.

Mase was studying me carefully, and I didn't want him to think for a minute that I was upset with him. He was doing this for me. He cared enough to put his own needs aside and be gentle with me. It made me love him even more.

"Do you understand?" he asked, his voice full of concern.

A real smile formed on my lips as I looked at him. "I understand. Thank you. Things like this only make me trust you more."

Mase

This was not how I wanted to spend my last night with Reese. I wasn't sure when I would get another weekend to come stay with her. I had spent most of the morning staring at the ceiling while I held her, thinking of ways to persuade her to come to Texas. I was ready to move her into my house. That's how far gone I was, and we hadn't even had sex yet.

Luckily, Tripp Newark Montgomery's fiancée, Bethy, wasn't one of the uptight Rosemary Beach females who made everything black-tie. She had worked at the Kerrington Club with her aunt for years. This party had been planned under her supervision, so we were all dressed for a party on the beach.

I glanced down at Reese, who was holding on to my arm tightly. She was wearing a bikini under her sundress, and I could see the straps peeking out. Swimsuits were the suggested attire. After the groundbreaking ceremony for Tripp's brand-new five-star hotel, everyone was moving to the Kerrington Club pool, which was more like a tropical island with waterfalls and palm trees.

"It seems like my wife can get you to do her bidding, too," Grant Carter said with a smirk, as he walked up to us. "Hello, Reese. Glad to see my brother-in-law has good taste."

"Hello, Mr. Carter," she said, her voice giving away how nervous she was.

Grant frowned. "You're dating Mase and having cookie breaks with my wife. You can call me Grant. Please." He turned his attention back to me. "You staying in town long?"

Reese tensed beside me but only for a second. If I wasn't so attuned to her every move, I would have missed it. "I have to leave tomorrow. I left things in a bit of a mess," I admitted.

Grant chuckled, and his eyes flicked over to my left. "Yeah, I hear you swooped in and stole Thad's date for the night. He's currently drinking heavily and has a woman on each arm. So he's recovering."

I didn't even bother looking. I didn't doubt Grant for a second. "Where's Harlow?" I asked, changing the subject.

"She's feeding Lila Kate. I offered to do it, but she said I was the one who needed to be out here showing my face, not her."

"I have to say, I like the relaxed atmosphere. I'm not sure Harlow could have gotten me to come if this were formal."

Grant chuckled like he didn't believe me.

A server appeared with a tray of champagne flutes. I took two and handed one to Reese. "You thirsty?"

She grinned and looked at the glass, then at me. "What is it?"

"Champagne," I replied, unable to take my eyes off her face. Every expression she made was something I wanted to etch into my memory.

"I've never had champagne before," she said softly.

"I think you'll like it. Just take a small sip."

She placed the glass to her lips, and her eyes stayed locked on me as she tasted the blush-colored drink. Her eyes lit with pleasure and excitement. She liked it. And watching her experience it was fucking amazing. It was just a drink, but she made everything an adventure. "It's really good. It tickles my nose."

There were several places I wanted to tickle her. But I kept that thought to myself. Glancing over, I realized I'd forgotten about Grant, but he'd moved on from us anyway.

"Hello, I'm Della. You must be Reese."

I turned back around to see Della Kerrington, Woods's wife, smiling at Reese. Della was a nice person. I felt safe with her approaching Reese. She hadn't come from this world, either, although she was now the wife of the owner of the Kerrington Club.

"Yes, I am. It's nice to meet you," Reese said, with less nerves this time. It seemed to be only men who made her withdraw.

"It's lovely to meet you, too. I've heard so many good things about you from Harlow."

Reese's eyes went wide, and she glanced over at me quickly before smiling back at Della. "Oh. Well, I enjoy working for Mrs. Carter. They're a really nice family."

Harlow would hate that Reese still felt she had to call her Mrs. Carter. I didn't correct her, though, although I could see the confusion flash in Della's eyes. She wasn't expecting Reese to be so formal about her relationship with my sister.

"Yes, they are," Della said, smiling. "I look forward to seeing more of you in the future." She gave me a knowing glance. "You two enjoy yourselves. I've got to go rescue my husband from Mr. Hobes. If you'll excuse me." She hurried toward Woods, who was listening to an older man talk and looking like he'd rather be anywhere else.

"She's beautiful," Reese said, as she watched Della walk away.

"I didn't notice," I replied, then tugged her closer to me. Thad was headed our way with his two dates, one on each side. I wasn't sure what his plan was, but I wasn't letting him say or do anything to embarrass Reese.

He also needed to understand: she was mine.

Thad's hair was tucked behind his ears, and his eyes weren't glassy or bloodshot from too much drink. The girls at his side were already in their bikinis. They had forgone the cover-ups or dresses, unlike everyone else.

Reese's hand tightened on my arm the second she noticed him. I tucked her against me and leveled a warning glare at Thad. He just grinned at me as if I was overreacting.

"Reese, Mase, hope you're enjoying yourselves," Thad said, as his stupid, dimpled grin flashed. I hoped Reese didn't have a thing for dimples.

"Yes, thank you. It's a beautiful spot for a hotel," Reese said sincerely.

"I hadn't planned on coming, but since my evening plans fell through, I figured I'd bring a couple of dates to entertain me," he said, with a wink, then did something to the girl on the right to cause her to squeal and giggle.

"I can see you're torn up about those failed plans. If you'll excuse us, I want to introduce Reese to Blaire and Rush," I said, placing a possessive hand on her lower back. I didn't wait for him to say anything else. I had seen Rush and Blaire arrive a few minutes ago, and I knew Blaire would be a safe person to talk to; plus, she was part of my family, so to speak. Rush and I both had fathers in the rock band Slacker Demon. Although

Rush grew up more in that life than I did, we understood what it was like to have fathers the rest of the world idolized.

Rush also wouldn't look at Reese like he wanted a taste. Because I was going to throttle Thad if I had to watch him lust over Reese another second.

Reese

When Mase introduced Rush Finlay, it clicked into place. Manning and Finlay. Rush was Dean Finlay's son. That's how Mase knew him. Their fathers. Wow.

While Mase didn't look like a rock god's son, Rush definitely did. From his pierced tongue, which flashed when he spoke, to the tattoos on his arms and neck, to the all-around swagger he possessed, Rush Finlay screamed Slacker Demon offspring.

His wife, Blaire, was the kind of beautiful who left you speechless for a moment because you weren't sure if she was real. The white-blond of her hair made her seem almost angelic. There was a kindness in her smile that made her seem even more heavenly, but then she opened her mouth, and a much thicker Southern twang than even Harlow's came out. I couldn't help but smile. She wasn't a model or a movie star, though that was the type of girl I expected to see Rush Finlay's arm wrapped around possessively. But then again, she was gorgeous enough to be both, so I didn't question it. She fit him. More so than I think anyone else could.

I talked with Blaire about Harlow and Lila Kate. She also asked me about Jimmy, since he'd given me her number after

134

her maid retired, but she never brought up me cleaning her house. In a way, I was glad, because that would only remind me of how much I didn't fit in here. But then, it also made me wonder if she had hired someone else. I really could use the job.

One thing that was becoming more difficult to ignore was the women who flirted with Mase. He didn't seem to notice, but even the servers gave him looks that were meant to let him know they were available.

If getting a woman was this easy for Mase . . . why was he with me?

⚙

Two hours later, the groundbreaking ceremony was complete, and the party had moved to the Kerrington Club. And unfortunately, now that the women were all walking around in their bikinis, they were even more flirty with Mase. Several had openly walked up to him and asked him to swim or dance. He had casually declined their offers, but it was as if I wasn't even standing there. I hadn't taken off my sundress yet, because I wasn't comfortable wearing a swimsuit in front of all those people. But I started thinking I might need to if I wanted to keep Mase's attention.

I spotted Blaire across the pool, and she was still wearing the blouse and short summery skirt she'd had on earlier. She wasn't strutting around in her swimsuit. She also didn't seemed bothered by the women who were looking at her husband with covetous glances.

But she was married to Rush.

I was on my first date with Mase.

"You want a drink?" Mase asked me. His hand slid around my waist as he bent down and whispered in my ear.

"Yes, please," I said, needing something to distract me.

"Stay here. I'll go brave the bar. More champagne? Or something else?"

I didn't want to stay here. Couldn't we wait for a server to walk around with one of those trays? But then I doubted he wanted the fruity drinks they were serving that way. "Champagne is fine," I replied.

He squeezed my side. "I'll be right back."

Just as I'd feared, women seized the opportunity and approached him as he walked away from me. He was polite and didn't seem interested, but it was still hard to watch. Because those girls wouldn't be nervous when he touched them. They'd have sex with him behind a palm tree out here if he wanted them to. That was what I had to compete with.

Besides, I had a twisted darkness inside my past that I would never be able to fully tell Mase about. They didn't have that kind of problem. They were free to enjoy their bodies and make men happy. I felt sick.

A blonde wrapped her arms around Mase and kissed his cheek. He gently pushed her away, but he continued to talk to her as he got our drinks. I couldn't watch this. I moved my attention to anywhere else. Harlow and Grant had already left with Lila Kate; they hadn't stayed at the party long. There was no one else I knew. Mase had introduced me to several people, but I didn't really know them.

I would not glance back at Mase. I was also considering taking off my sundress. But these women had bodies much nicer than mine. They were thin, with no added padding in their bottoms. And their boobs were all nice and round and perfectly positioned on their chests. Not too big or too small.

Taking off my dress might be a bad idea after all. At least, Mase wouldn't be able to see exactly how imperfect my body was. God, I hated this feeling. I never compared myself with other women. At least, not in the past. Now here I was, doing it.

My gaze went back to Mase. He was now holding two drinks and headed my way. The blonde was gone. He seemed annoyed. I hoped it wasn't because he was here with me but could be having sex right now with a number of willing, beautiful women.

I could lose him.

So very easily.

And I'd just gotten him.

When he finally reached me, he handed me the champagne. "Once you finish that, are you ready to go? I'm ready to have you alone. I've done my duty and shown my face here."

I had the urge to throw back the flute and down the pink bubbly drink. I was ready to leave, too—before Mase got an offer he couldn't refuse. I was thankful for his ranch out in Texas. I didn't imagine there were gorgeous, model-thin heiresses throwing themselves at him there.

"Yes. I'd like to go when you're ready," I admitted.

Mase studied my face a moment, then took the champagne from my hand. "I'll buy you a bottle at the store if you want more. Let's go," he said, putting the flute down on the table nearest to us and leaving his untouched small glass of amber liquid there, too.

His hand settled on my lower back, and he led me through the crowd as he took us out to where the valet waited.

Once we were in the truck, Mase reached over and took my hand, threading his fingers through mine. "Thanks for coming with me tonight. I only went because Harlow thought I should show my face since I was in town. She's friends with Bethy and Tripp. I was glad I had you with me. Made the night bearable."

That man and his words. It almost made me forget how hard it was to watch women flirt with him with every breath he took. He didn't flirt back, though. But I didn't see Mase as a flirter. It wasn't his style. Didn't mean he didn't enjoy their attention. How could he not? They were beautiful and willing.

"I liked meeting your friends," I told him.

He squeezed my hand. "They liked meeting you."

I wanted to ask him how he knew the blonde who had hugged him and kissed him. But I didn't. I kept my mouth shut.

"Do you want me to stop and get more champagne?" he asked, with a trace of humor in his voice.

I shook my head no and laughed.

"I like to hear you laugh. You didn't do much of that tonight," he said, as his thumb began caressing my hand. "You laughed more today when it was just us."

"I was too busy taking it all in."

"Thanks for not taking off that little dress of yours."

Why did he say that? Was he worried about how I'd look without it?

"If you'd taken it off, I'm afraid we would have left even earlier, because I'd have been thrown out. I don't like the idea of another man looking at what's mine."

Whoa. OK. I was his? Oh . . . wow.

"I kept thinking about how I'd react if you wanted to swim. I was trying to come up with excuses to keep that sweet ass covered up."

The ache between my legs started again. Hearing him call my butt a sweet ass excited me, apparently. I liked how it felt when he touched my bottom. I squirmed in my seat, and his hand tightened around mine.

We didn't say anything else. By the time he parked the truck at my apartment, the air felt hot, and I was breathing heavily. Glancing at Mase, I saw his jaw clenched tightly. His hand still held mine firmly.

When he cut off the engine and finally let my hand go, he jerked open his door and was out so fast you would have thought it was on fire. I watched him as he took long strides to my side of the truck and threw open the door. I started to get out, but then he was backing me up, crowding me in.

His nostrils flared as he got close to me, and his eyes flashed a needy look I understood. My entire body felt feverish, but his hands only touched my hips. His head lowered to my ear, and he ran his nose down and back up my neck. "God, you smell so good. I could smell you for fucking ever and be happy."

I grabbed his shoulders and held on. Words like that coming from Mase Manning made a girl light-headed.

"When we get inside, I want to take this dress off. Let me see you in this swimsuit. Please. I won't ask for anything more. Just let me look at you and touch you . . . Just a little."

My body felt so fevered I was ready to rip everything off right now for him, but I knew the moment I did, I would panic. Reality would set in. I managed a nod and let him lead me out of the truck. He pressed a hot, hard kiss to my lips, more aggressive than the ones that had come before. I held on while he took that kiss. It wasn't one of his easy, sweet ones, but it was exciting.

When he tore his mouth off mine, he muttered a curse, then led me to the apartment door and unlocked it before ushering me inside quickly.

Before I could catch my breath, his hands were taking the bottom of my sundress in his hands. "I'm just going to take this off. That's all. Just need to see you," he whispered close to my ear, but he didn't move until I nodded my head.

When I gave him the go-ahead, he lifted the dress slowly. Once it was over my bottom, he groaned. I lifted my arms, and he pulled it up and off. I didn't move. I knew what he was looking at, and I closed my eyes tightly. I hadn't looked at my butt in the mirror in a long time. There was a good chance it was dimply. I really hoped it wasn't. I walked a lot still. I was sure walking all my life had been one reason my bottom wasn't massive.

His fingertip brushed the underside of my left butt cheek, and I gasped, but I didn't move. He was touching me. Barely.

"There's a freckle right here. I love this freckle. Best fucking freckle in the world," he said in a thick, deep voice.

Then I heard him move, and I glanced back to see him going down on his knees. I started to turn, and his hands grabbed my waist and held me still.

"Please, Reese. Don't. Not yet," he begged. So I stayed still.

His warm breath hovered over my skin, and I trembled. Knowing his face was so close to any part of me was exciting, but this was almost too much. Then his lips grazed the same spot he'd touched, and I released a strangled cry from the shock and pleasure.

"Just had to kiss it," he said, pressing his lips against that spot again. Then his hands slid up over my bottom, and he squeezed gently. "Swear, Reese, this ass is perfection," he said in a reverent tone. "So fucking glad you didn't wear this swimsuit in front of other men tonight. This is my ass. I don't want anyone else seeing this juicy little piece of heaven."

I closed my eyes tightly. Was I really letting him kneel behind me and play with my bottom? My heart was racing, and the fever in my body was at an all-time high.

Mase moved some of the swimsuit covering my butt over until more of my cheek was bared and pressed another kiss to me. Oh, God, he was kissing my bottom.

"You even smell good down here. I can smell how this excites you. It mixes well with that sweet cream cinnamon smell that clings to you."

I really needed something to hold on to before I melted into a puddle. My knees buckled a little, and Mase's hands tightened on my waist as he stood back up behind me. He didn't cover my bared cheek back up, and he slid his body up against mine.

He kissed my shoulder, then brushed my hair back off my neck and ran his nose over the curve of my ear. "I don't want to do anything you aren't ready for. But I want to touch you. That's all. Nothing more. Are you ready for that? If not, it's OK. I can just look." It sounded like that last part was ripped from him unwillingly.

All those beautiful women throwing themselves at him, and he wanted me. He chose me. I could let him touch me some. I wasn't panicked yet, and right now, all I could think about was Mase and how he felt. How he made me feel. "Yes," I said, sounding as if I was completely out of breath.

He ran a finger down my neck and wrapped a strand of hair around his finger. "Thank you. For trusting me. You don't have to, and knowing that you like my touch is the most fucking beautiful thing anyone's ever given me."

He didn't start groping at my body. Instead, we stood there, as he played with my hair and continued running his nose and lips over my neck and ear. I slowly leaned back into him as my body relaxed under his gentle caress.

"Your hair is like playing with silk," he whispered. "And your skin." He ran a hand down my bare arm and slid that same hand over the butt cheek he had left exposed. "I've decided I'm obsessed with silk," he added.

I started to squirm when his hand slid back up my body, circling around to the front and stopping on my stomach. "Turn around, and let me see you," he said, stepping back from me.

I was breathing heavily, and I knew he could see it. But facing him made it more real. I would be able to see him as he looked at me.

His gaze ran down my body slowly, then back up again. There was a worshipful look on his face that made me feel cherished. Important. Protected.

Those were three things I had never felt.

I would not cry.

He stepped closer and placed his fingertips on my stomach, tracing my belly button. Then both hands were on me, as he moved them up slowly until he grazed the bottoms of my breasts. With one finger, he traced my cleavage and dipped into the crevice between my breasts. "I want these bare and in my hands," he said, as he lifted his eyes to meet mine in a silent request.

I inhaled sharply but not from fear. I wanted that, too. The areas around my nipples were in pain, they ached so badly. "OK," I said, knowing he wouldn't do anything until I said he could.

He slid his arms around me and untied the halter top and the back of my suit. It fell away and drifted to the floor, and my boobs bounced free.

"Fuck, those are amazing," he breathed, as his hands cupped them and his thumb played with my nipples. "Can I taste them?" He sounded like he was begging again.

"Yes," I said breathily, reaching out to grab his arms in case my knees completely gave out.

Mase growled and lowered his head. Then his tongue flicked at my right breast. He made a pleased sound in his chest before he pulled an entire nipple into his mouth and sucked on it.

My legs went weak, and I cried out as pleasure rocketed through my body.

Mase picked me up before I collapsed on the floor and carried me over to the sofa, sinking down with me firmly in his lap. He kissed my lips as I panted, still reeling from his mouth on my chest.

One of his hands still kneaded my breasts, and I wanted his mouth there again. "Can I taste them again?"

I nodded, wanting to shove his head back down to my breasts and never let him up.

Mase's warm mouth pulled the other nipple into his mouth, and I cried out again as my hands fisted in his hair. I worried that I might hurt him, but I had to hold on to something. His hands held my breasts as he kissed and even nibbled on them. I whimpered and cried out his name as I held his head against me. I wanted this to last forever.

The ache between my legs was so intense now that I had to squirm and squeeze my legs together. Something to make it stop. I needed it to stop.

"Spread your legs. I'll make it better," Mase said in a demanding tone that startled me.

I wasn't sure what to do. If I spread my legs, I knew he was going to touch me there. My body was saying yes, it needed it, but my brain was telling me it would hurt. I was dirty there.

"Please, baby. Let me take care of that pussy. It's so wet I can smell you, Reese. It's driving me crazy. I'll even kiss it if you'll let me. Anything, baby. I'll do anything for you. Fucking anything." He sounded desperate.

I loved him.

I didn't want to lose him to some woman who didn't need to be begged.

I wanted to make him happy.

I pushed the fear back and opened my legs just enough so that his hand slipped between them. He gently pulled my legs open more, and I held my breath as his hand slid down my thigh.

I fought the panic. I tried to keep it back. This was Mase. He was good to me. I loved him.

Then a finger slid inside my bikini bottoms, and the ache

vanished as the memories crashed over me. I was going to be sick.

I couldn't do this. Oh, God, I couldn't do this.

I shoved his hand away and jumped up and ran to the bathroom. I couldn't get sick.

Turning on the faucet, I splashed cold water on my face several times and told myself over and over that I was OK.

Mase

I had never hated anyone as much as I hated myself at that moment. The only man I hated more was her goddamn step-father. Afraid to touch her, I stood behind her as she splashed cold water on her face and chanted in a soft voice, "You're OK. It's OK. You're OK. It's OK."

With every "OK," my chest felt like it was being ripped wide open.

My head had been telling me to stop. I was pushing for too much. But I couldn't stop touching her. She felt so fucking good. Seeing her face as I gave her pleasure was like crack. I wanted more and more of it.

I had scared her in the end, though. I was asking for too much.

But I wasn't willing to lose her. I'd do whatever the hell she wanted me to. I just didn't want to lose her.

After what seemed like an eternity, she turned off the water and reached for a towel to dry her face. She took several deep breaths before dropping the towel and turning to face me.

I had started to apologize when her mouth puckered up into a pout, and then she burst into tears. *Shit!*

Without waiting for her, I pulled her into my arms. I didn't know what to say. I didn't know if she was crying because of me and what I'd done or if she was crying because of her own reaction.

"It's OK, sweetheart. I got you. It's OK," I said, trying to soothe her. I hated the sobs that caused her body to shake in my arms.

"I'm so-o-o-orry," she cried loudly.

Fuck that. I picked her up, carried her to the bed, and sat down with her still in my arms. I leaned against the headboard and held her like a baby, cuddling her to my chest. "I told you not to apologize to me. Ever. It's me who's sorry, Reese."

She grabbed my T-shirt in her fist and cried harder.

"I'm br-r-roo-o-ken," she sobbed. "You do-o-on't ha-ave to se-e-ttle for br-r-r-ooo-oken." She let out a loud wail like she was mourning a death.

God, I swore, if I ever found the man who did this to her, he would pay.

I tucked her head under my chin and tightened my hold on her. "You are perfect. So perfect that you take my breath away. I'm completely obsessed with you. You're all I see anymore, Reese. Nothing about you is broken. Please, don't let me ever hear you say that again. I want you to see yourself the way I do. This breathtaking beauty who has me so completely fascinated. She's a fighter. She's strong. She's fun, and she is kind and honest. She doesn't judge others. She accepts people for who they are. She doesn't expect anything but gives beauty to the world around her freely. That is who I see, Reese. That is who you are. See that, too, sweetheart. Please, see that, too."

Her crying dissolved into little hiccups, but her grip on my shirt only intensified. I watched as she finally tilted her head back to look up at me with red, swollen eyes. Even now, she was still amazing.

"You think that . . . about me?"

I pressed a kiss to her forehead. "Yes, I do."

She started to say something, and her body tensed. I knew she was just now realizing that she was still topless. I shifted quickly, pulled my shirt off, and slipped it on her. I didn't want her to move. Not yet.

She helped by putting her arms through the holes. It was too big on her, but seeing her covered up in my shirt stroked my possessive beast.

"Thank you," she said, wrapping her arms around her stomach like she was cuddling with my shirt. I liked that, too.

"I asked for too much tonight. This was my fault. I will be more careful in the future. I swear. Please, don't stop trusting me," I said, needing her to believe me.

She frowned. "You always asked me. I could have said no. It isn't your fault."

But it was. "Next time you want more, you will have to ask for it. I won't push again. I swear to you."

Then we would both know she wanted it.

She sighed and covered her face with both hands. "I wish I wasn't like this."

I did, too. But for different reasons. I wished she had no nightmares in her past. I hated that she suffered from something so horrific. Hell, I hated that she suffered at all.

"Will you hold me tonight while we sleep again?"

"You never have to ask that, Reese. The answer is always yes."

⌘

Late the next morning, I left Reese standing at the door wearing my shirt. It was the hardest thing I'd had to do. I didn't like leaving her. I wanted her with me.

"Wear my shirt at night. I like knowing that you have something of mine when I'm gone."

She had nodded and let me kiss her before I took my duffel bag and headed back to Texas.

Reese

Jimmy was at my door with two cappuccinos on Monday morning. I was so glad to see him that I hugged him tightly before taking my java goodness from him. "You're back. Are you better? Can you sleep?"

He beamed at me. He loved the attention. "Yeah, I'm good. I had a few rough nights, but I'm better. I see they took the tape down."

I nodded. I tried not to think about the shooting. From the little I had seen on the news, I knew that Jacob was being held without bail. He would be tried for murder. And Melanie's parents had come to take her body back to Iowa to bury her.

"I'm glad you're back."

"Missed me, did ya? Good. I heard you broke Thad's heart while I was gone. But since it was over Mase Manning, I'm gonna say that was a smart move, sugar. Thad might be pretty, and his ass might be the tightest thing I've ever seen, but he likes to dip his dick in a new woman every damn night. Not your type at all."

I frowned, then laughed at his description of Thad. "More info than I needed, but OK."

"Drink that cappuccino, darling, because you're gonna

need it. I heard that the wicked witch of the beach is back.
She arrived from Paris late last night. Prepare yourself for this.
Nannette is an evil, evil bitch. She's also gonna take one look at
you and get pissy. She doesn't deal well when there's a female
hotter than she is, and baby, you are smoking."

I would be lying if I said I wasn't curious about Nan. She
was Mase's sister. But I also had to tell her about her mirror.
Mase hadn't brought it up again, but I knew I had to tell Nan
what had happened. Every time I cleaned that room, I saw that
empty space and dreaded having to tell her what I had done.

There was a good chance Nan would fire me. I was preparing myself for that, too. But I was going to call Blaire Finlay
this afternoon and see about cleaning her house. If I was fired
from Nan's, then at least I wouldn't hurt from the pay cut.

I grabbed my backpack and slipped it up my arm and followed Jimmy out to his car. "How did you hear about Thad?"
I asked.

Jimmy grinned like he knew the best secret in the world.
"I got a call from Mase last night. He wanted to make sure I
was home and I would be picking you up for work. He also
explained that he'd need to know the next time I was out of
town or couldn't take you to work. He didn't want Thad to be
my first call. He said he would make arrangements." Jimmy
wiggled his eyebrows. "So naturally, after that very intimidat-
ing call, I called Blaire and asked her what the scoop was. She
didn't know the details, so she called Harlow, who, of course,
knew. Then Blaire called me back and filled me in."

I couldn't help but laugh. "I can't believe you called Blaire
Finlay and asked her what she knew."

Jimmy laughed and cranked the car. "Blaire was my girl

before she was a Finlay. Even married to hot, sexy-as-hell, do-me-now Rush Finlay, she's still my girl."

The way Rush looked at his wife, I couldn't imagine he would like anyone calling Blaire "my girl"—even Jimmy, who apparently lusted over Rush's body regardless of his friend being married to him.

"Now, tell me, any yummy deets you can share about Mase?"

I thought about last night and how good he had made me feel. Even after I lost it and messed up the moment, he had been so gentle and sweet.

"I love him." There, I'd said it. I had to say to it someone.

Jimmy slammed on the brakes and looked at me. Thank God, we weren't out of the parking lot yet. "You did not just say that."

I shrugged. "I can't help it. I won't tell him. But he makes it impossible not to love him. He's just . . . just what every girl dreams of. He makes everything right when it all seems wrong."

Jimmy laid his head back against the seat and groaned in frustration. "Baby girl, what are you thinking? You can't fall in love with Mase Manning. He doesn't even live here, for starters. Long-distance relationships don't work. He's a grown, very healthy man. He's gonna need to get his groove on, and he's gonna have women throwing themselves at him over in Texas. You can't love him. He's the kind you enjoy and appreciate. Not love."

My good mood evaporated. A sick knot formed in my stomach.

Was Jimmy right? Probably. He knew so much more about relationships than I did.

Did Mase have to have sex? I hadn't given him sex. Oh, God.

"He's probably got a woman in Texas, maybe even a couple he gets his goodies from. You gotta know that, sweetie. And I'm betting you didn't have sex with him, did you? Don't answer that, I know you didn't. I would have seen it all over your face if you had. So that means he went back to Texas horny. He's gonna get it somewhere, Reese. Those are the facts, and I don't want you hurt."

Hurt? I was devastated. "But I love him," was all I could say.

Jimmy reached over and squeezed my thigh. "I'm sorry. I don't want you to be upset. But you don't need to be blind to this. Has he told you he loves you?"

I shook my head no.

Jimmy sighed. "Girl, what am I gonna do with you? Love is one of them things you gotta be careful with. Guard yourself. I still got that friend we can double-date with."

Mase had said I was his. He didn't want anyone else to see me in my swimsuit. I didn't know if that meant we were exclusive, because apparently, I didn't know a lot. But I didn't want to go out with someone else. And I didn't think Mase would want me to.

If I was his, he wouldn't sleep with someone else . . . would he?

The Mase I knew wouldn't do that. I didn't believe he would have sex with someone else. He hadn't told me he loved me, but he had said things that made me feel like I belonged to him . . . and like he belonged to me. Like he wanted to be mine.

"He said I was his," I told Jimmy.

Jimmy's eyebrows shot up. "Really? He said that? Like how did he say it? Give it to me word for word. I mean, I know he didn't want Thad taking you anywhere, but I figured he was protecting you from the man-whore who had his eye on you. I didn't think it was because he was laying claim just yet."

I didn't want to share my private time with Mase with anyone else. But I also didn't want to make a mistake and end up so completely broken that I couldn't ever recover. "He said he was glad I hadn't worn my swimsuit in front of everyone at the party, because he didn't want another man looking at what was his."

Jimmy let out a low whistle. "Maybe you better not date anyone else right now. Maybe I misjudged this. I don't want an angry cowboy coming to Rosemary Beach ready to kill someone. Let's just be careful, OK? Try not to love him too hard. Guard your heart, if you can."

I had given Mase Manning my heart already. I didn't have anything left to guard. But I didn't tell Jimmy that.

Mase

Cordelia's truck was in my drive when I got back from eating lunch with my parents. Not what I wanted to deal with today, or ever. I needed to get my wallet and head to the stockyards. I was already running late.

I opened the door to the house and cursed myself for leaving it unlocked. Apparently, I was going to have to start locking up, because my neighbor was refusing to listen to me and go away.

"Cord, where you at?" I called out, when I opened the door to an empty living room.

"Come find me," she called out teasingly.

Shit. Not good.

I threw my work gloves down and toed off my boots to keep from tracking mud into the house. Then I headed to the bedroom to kick out my visitor.

Sure enough, there she was, naked on my bed. I was going to have to wash the sheets to get her smell off them. I was tired and done with this shit. She had taken it a step too far this time.

"Get your clothes on and leave."

"Don't, Mase. Look at me. You wanted this once. We were

so good together. I want you. So bad," she said, opening her legs and slipping her hand between them and playing with herself.

"You've gone too far, Cordelia. I want you out of my house. If I need to call my momma to come get you to leave, I will," I threatened. I figured the idea of my momma finding her naked in my bed was enough to get any woman up and moving.

"Mase, don't do this. Please. I miss you. I need you so bad. I want you to fuck me however you want me. I'll give you anything you want. Let me suck your dick. You can gag me with it like you love to do."

"Stop!" My angry shout finally shut her up. "I'm in love with someone. She's all I want. All I'm ever gonna want. So I need you to get your clothes and get out of my house, Cord. Now." I turned and left her there, not liking the image of her on my bed. That should be Reese there. Sweet, sexy Reese.

I would need to get new sheets and a new mattress before I brought Reese here. Get rid of what I'd fucked Cordelia and a few other women on. Reese was too good to be where they'd been. She was special.

Cord's footsteps finally alerted me that she'd given up. When I looked up, she was carrying her clothes and strutting naked through my house. Damn, did she not have any shame at all? I turned my back to her so she wouldn't think I was looking at her in any way and enjoying this shit.

When the door slammed behind her and I heard her truck start up, I finally let out a sigh of relief and headed to my bedroom to strip my damn sheets. Luckily, my mother made sure I always had two sets of sheets. She said you always needed a backup. Like always, my mother was right.

Once I was done, I knew I'd wasted too much time. I would have to go to the stockyard first thing the next day. I had a man coming at four to look at a horse I was selling. I needed to get things cleaned up from our morning routine before he got here.

Major was walking up to the house from my parents' place when I came back outside. "You not going to the stockyards?" he called out from down the hill.

"No, I'm waiting until tomorrow morning. Got that quarter I'm selling that I need to get cleaned up from her run this morning."

Major nodded. "I'm headed out, then. Got to be in San Antonio tomorrow. Dad wants to meet with me."

I didn't envy him. His relationship with his dad had been shit ever since he slept with his stepmother last year. "Good luck," was my only response.

He shot me a bird and headed back toward my parents' house.

Grinning, I went to my truck and climbed inside.

I still couldn't believe the stupid fuck had slept with his stepmom. Even if she was only three years older than him. Last I heard, she wasn't his stepmom anymore. And the prenup she'd signed left her high and dry.

Reese

I had been very careful to stay downstairs and be quiet while cleaning. I didn't want to wake up the woman all of Rosemary Beach had taught me to fear. But today I actually had something to clean; she was messy.

I spent more than an hour cleaning up what looked like a bottle of wine that had exploded all over the kitchen floor. Shards of glass littered the floor, and dry, sticky drink was all over the place. The cabinets, floors, counters—everywhere. Once I managed to get that mess cleaned up, I was able to clean the dishes and glasses I found littered around the downstairs.

Then I found piles of clothes on the laundry-room floor. Most of them looked clean, and I was sure most of them needed to be dry-cleaned. It looked like she had just dumped the contents of her luggage onto the floor. It took me another hour to sort the dry-cleaning from the regular laundry, and then I began washing a load of whites.

Once the downstairs was sparkling and I had the washing under control, it was past noon. I decided I could keep quiet and work on the rooms farthest from hers on the second floor. She would be asleep on the third floor. I knew which room was hers.

The bedrooms that had remained untouched were easy. I

just had to dust and sweep and mop. Same routine. When I got to the game room, I cringed, thinking of the mirror I would have to tell her about. There were empty glasses in here, too. It looked like she might already know her mirror was missing. She must have had people in here. Scraps of food were scattered on plates, and the dregs of different alcoholic drinks were left in glasses. Garbage littered the floor.

The worst was the used condom in the corner beside the leather sofa. *Gross.* I put on the gloves I had bought when I had stitches and got a large wad of toilet paper before picking it up and disposing of the condom. At least the user had tied it off.

Once I finished in the game room, it was almost three. I was normally done by three, but I still had the upstairs to do. And she was still sleeping.

I went back downstairs, walked all the trash out, and put the recycling in the correct bins, then came back inside and was considering reorganizing her pantry when I heard footsteps on the stairs. Finally.

I straightened my clothes and tucked my loose hair behind my ears. When Nannette walked into the kitchen, she saw me and scowled, then tossed her hair over her shoulder. As I'd predicted, she was stunning. Long strawberry-blond hair hung down her back. She was barely covered up, in a short, silky black nightgown that showcased her perfect pale skin.

"You the housecleaner?" she asked, sounding pissed.

"Yes, ma'am," I replied.

"Why are you still here? It's after three. It always take you this fucking long?"

"I'm finished with everything but upstairs. I was waiting for you to wake up."

She scrunched her nose at me. "Well, go clean it. I'm awake. Stop standing there gawking at me."

I needed to tell her about the mirror, but she didn't look like she wanted to chat just yet. So I hurried upstairs quickly and focused on cleaning everything I could. I didn't want her to have one complaint. Other than the mirror.

It took me two more hours upstairs. She had left a wake of disaster in her room. It made the rest of her house look positively spotless.

When I was satisfied, I headed back downstairs to see her curled up on the sofa with the remote in her hand and a cup of coffee on the table beside her. She looked more awake now.

"Took you long enough. You're slow. Speed it up, or you're gone," she snapped.

"I'm sorry. I will," I replied, thinking it was unfair that she thought I could go any faster.

She rolled her eyes and dismissed me with a flick of her hand. I had to tell her about the mirror, though. It would keep me up nights worrying until I did.

"While you were gone, there was an accident when I was cleaning the windows in the game room. I fell, and the mirror beside the window overlooking the Gulf came down with me. It shattered, and the frame broke. I will pay for it out of my paycheck until it's completely covered. I'm really sorry—"

"The hell you will. You'll pay me right now. That mirror cost more than five thousand dollars. It came from Paris, as did most of the furnishings in this house."

I didn't have five thousand dollars. I had two thousand saved up right now, but that was it. How did one mirror cost so much? I hadn't expected this. "I'm sorry. I don't have that.

I can give you two thousand right now and then work until it's paid for. That's the best I can do," I explained, hoping this woman had some form of empathy in her.

She glared at me; those green eyes were taking no prisoners. I was in trouble. Serious trouble. "No, you won't. I'll contact the agency and have them pay me back. They sent me a moron, so they can pay for it."

I had to sign a consent form when I started working for them that any damage that occurred was my responsibility. I just never imagined I would break a five-thousand-dollar mirror. "They won't cover it. They'll make me do it. It's my responsibility. All I have is—"

"Not even half. I heard you the first time. Go whine to someone else. I want my money, so figure it out, or I'll call the police and let them deal with your thieving ass."

The police. Oh, God, I was going to go to jail over this. "I didn't steal it. It broke," I started to explain.

"Shut up! Get out of my house. There is no proof that it was broken. It's not here. I want my five thousand for it, or you can tell the cops you didn't steal it. Now, get out of my house."

I didn't say anything else. She looked ready to explode if I spoke to her again. This was not what I had imagined. Not at all. I thought she'd be mad, but I thought she'd at least let me pay her back.

I hurried to the door and got my backpack before running to the main road. Off her property. I had a lesson tonight with Dr. Munroe, but I couldn't go. I needed to go home and figure out what to do. I called the professor and told him I wasn't feeling well, then walked home slowly.

Mase

When ten thirty rolled around and I still hadn't gotten a call from Reese, I called her instead. Something was wrong. She'd have called me by now if everything was fine. The phone rang until it went to voice mail. I hung up and tried again. The same thing.

I tried to tell myself not to panic, and I dialed Jimmy's number.

He answered on the third ring. "Hel—"

"Have you seen Reese?" I asked, not letting him finish his greeting.

"Yeah, she was walking home later than usual, and I gave her a ride back. She said she had a headache and was going to get a shower and go to bed."

A headache was normal. I didn't need to panic, but dammit, I wanted to know she was OK. Not hearing her voice didn't sit well with me. "Go check on her. She's not answering her phone, and I need to know she's OK. She could be sick."

Jimmy sighed. "I am assuming this command also means you will be staying on the phone with me while I do your bidding."

I didn't even care that he was being a smart-ass. I just

162

wanted to know that Reese was OK. "Yeah, that's what it means."

"Fine. But if she's sleeping, this is going to wake her up."

I'd thought about that, but I couldn't not know. I kept imagining her sick in the bathroom, too weak to call someone, or passed out on the floor. My fears were getting more exaggerated by the second.

"You sure are protective over her. You'd think the two of you were in a serious relationship," he said in an amused tone.

"We are in a serious, very exclusive relationship. Did she not tell you that?"

Jimmy cleared his throat. "She wasn't sure what you were in. But she did tell me she couldn't double-date with me because she didn't think you'd like that."

Damn right I wouldn't like it. What did Reese think all that was this weekend? I came to town just to stop her from dating someone else. I made my interest very clear, over and over. "She thought right," was my only response. This wasn't a conversation I needed to have with Jimmy.

"I guess if you're not getting any on the side, then—"

"Jimmy, are you trying to find out if I'm fucking other women while I'm in Texas? Because if that is what this is and you're trying to protect Reese, then understand something: I don't want anyone but Reese. Ever. So stop trying to rile me up, and go check on my woman. Now."

Jimmy chuckled. "Well, all right, then. I can do that."

I breathed a sigh of relief. She wasn't thinking of dating other people. Jimmy just wanted to see if I was. I'd be pissed at him if it wasn't for the fact that he cared about her. He was just trying to watch out for her. I liked that.

I waited while Jimmy walked over to Reese's apartment and knocked on the door. "Reese, honey. If you're awake, could you open up? I got an angry cowboy on my phone interrupting my soaps."

I waited while I listened to Jimmy knock again.

"I hear the latch," Jimmy said, and the panic slowly started to ebb.

"Hey," her soft voice said from inside her apartment.

"You wanna talk to him?" Jimmy asked.

I heard the muffled sound of them whispering with a hand over the receiver. I hated it. Something was wrong. I was going to have to leave shit here again and go back to Rosemary Beach.

"Hey, sorry. I was asleep. It was a long day." Reese's voice came over the phone, thick with sleep. She wasn't lying. She'd been in bed. She was OK.

"Do you feel sick? Have Jimmy check your temperature," I said, feeling anxious that something was off.

"I'm fine. No fever, I promise. I'll call you tomorrow. I just needed to sleep tonight. But I'm not sick. I don't feel sick."

Something was wrong. I could feel it. "OK. Sleep, then, baby. I'll want to hear your voice in the morning, though. I won't be able to focus until I know you're better."

"I'll call," she assured me.

"Good night. Sweet dreams," I whispered, just before ending the call.

Fuck, I wasn't going to get any sleep now. Something was wrong, and she wasn't going to tell me what it was. I had sold the quarter horse today, but I had to be here when the buyer came to load it up tomorrow. He was also bringing the check so we could finalize the paperwork. Then I had to go to the stockyards and get some cattle. I should have gone yesterday. As it was, I was behind on shit.

But Reese needed me, and I couldn't be there. Another reason I wanted her here. Hell, I couldn't tell her that yet, though. She wasn't even ready to let me touch her pussy.

Throwing my phone down, I went to the fridge to get a beer. I had a long night ahead of me, and if I started thinking about Reese's pussy, it was just going to get longer.

Reese

I hadn't slept a wink after Jimmy came knocking on my door. Hearing Mase's voice and his concern had sent me into a fit of tears. Then I'd sat up and thought of every way possible I could make money, and fast. When I got my paycheck this week, it would give me twenty-eight hundred dollars total to my name. I would still need twenty-two hundred more.

I was afraid to try to get a night job waiting tables. When I got stressed or panicky, I still had trouble making out words. And my writing wasn't so good yet. I doubted I'd even be able to fill out the application. I had watched the sunrise, knowing I was just going to have to see how this played out. If she reported the mirror stolen, then they couldn't arrest me without proof. And I had proof of a sliced-open hand to hold up my side of the story.

The most a judge would do was make me pay her back, which was what I had already told her I would do. I knew I had to call Mase this morning. He was worried last night, but I just couldn't talk to him yet.

This whole mess was too upsetting. If I told him about what his sister was threatening to do, I was afraid he'd think I wanted him to pay her back for me. I couldn't let him do that or think that I would want that. This was my problem to deal with, not his.

I pressed his number, and it barely rang once before he answered.

"Good morning. Are you feeling better?" His voice made all the bad stuff plaguing me fade away. I missed him. I loved our nightly talks. Last night, I had wanted to talk to him, but I knew I couldn't. He could tell I was upset, and I couldn't hide it from him.

"Yes. I'm much better. Thank you. Sorry about last night," I replied.

"You being OK is all I'm worried about. Although I won't lie, I missed your voice reading to me last night. Hard to sleep without that."

I smiled for the first time since the awful meeting with Nan yesterday. He made me happy, even when things sucked. "That normally doesn't happen to me. But if it ever happens again, I promise to call before I go to sleep. I should have thought of calling you earlier and letting you know." Trying to sound normal was not easy. But I was doing the best I could.

"I'll let you get to work. Have a good day, baby."

I said good-bye and hung up, letting the warm feeling I got when he called me "baby" stay with me most of the morning.

❖

It was almost noon when I got the call from the cleaning agency. I had been fired. Nan had called them, and they wanted no connection with me. I was to come pick up my check and not report for the other two houses I had scheduled for that week.

I managed to finish cleaning the rest of the Carters' house that afternoon without breaking down.

I was going to be fine. I would call Blaire Finlay. Two houses would pay the bills. I wouldn't have any left over for extras or savings, so paying Nan back was going to be difficult. I had to find one more house to clean, at least, or another job.

Before I went home today, I was going to cut Nan a check for two thousand four hundred dollars. That was all I had right now. I wouldn't think about the rent just yet; I would worry about that next week. Right now, I needed to show that I was trying to pay for the mirror. I didn't want the cops coming after me.

The idea of facing Nan again was terrifying. However, when I finally got to her house, there were two cars parked outside, Nan's expensive little sports car and a black SUV. Having company could be a good thing. Surely she wouldn't be nasty in front of guests.

After giving myself a pep talk, I went up the front steps and rang the doorbell. I would give her the check, apologize again, and promise more money as soon as possible. Then I would leave. I could do this.

The door swung open sooner than I'd expected, and Nan's expression immediately turned into a disgusted sneer. "What are you doing here? I called the agency and had you fired. Do I need to call the cops, too?"

I went over what I had practiced in my head. "Here is a check with everything I have right now. I'll get you more as soon as I can. I'm really sorry about the mirror," I said, my voice only cracking once from nerves.

Rush Finlay walked up behind Nan. He wasn't smiling. What was he doing here?

"Nan? What's going on? Did you just say you had—" He stopped and looked at me. "It's Reese, correct?" I nodded. "Did you have Reese fired?"

"She stole a five-thousand-dollar mirror from my house! Yes, I had her fired. This is a check for not even half of it, and she thinks that makes it OK," Nan spat out.

Rush didn't look like he believed her. He turned back to me. "Reese, did you steal a mirror?"

I shook my head. "No. I did break it, though. I fell. It was an accident. I explained, but—"

"She's lying! She's the cleaning lady, Rush! God! Do you always have to take everyone else's side over mine? I've been gone for months, and this is what I get as a welcome home? A thieving housecleaner and my brother once again taking other people's sides against me?" She was yelling now. But the fact that she'd called Rush her brother confused me. How was Rush her brother? Mase was her brother, but Rush and Mase weren't brothers to each other.

"She brought you a check and is promising to bring you more when she can. Does that sound like someone who stole your mirror? No, it doesn't. Calm the fuck down, and think about this shit before you react. You're not ten goddamn years old anymore, Nan. Grow up." Rush was clearly annoyed.

"I'm going to go. I'll be back with the rest of the money as soon as I can," I said again, then hurried down the steps.

I probably should have stuck around and continued to defend myself. There was a good chance Rush might start to believe her, and then I wouldn't get that job working at his house. I would have to wait to call Blaire about the job. At least

I had a witness who saw that I'd paid her some for the mirror and promised to pay more soon.

It was an eight-mile walk home from here. I had enough time to think about what I would do the rest of the week since I no longer had houses to clean.

Mase

My phone rang as I was pulling into the house after a long day at the stockyards.

It was Rush.

"Hello," I said, not used to getting calls from him.

"Nan's back home," he said, not sounding real happy about it. Couldn't say I blamed him, but then, I thought he loved his sister.

"Yeah," I said, wondering what this shit had to do with me.

"You know anything about a mirror at Nan's house?"

Shit! I had forgotten about the mirror. And Nan being home. *Motherfucker.* Reese would have gone to clean yesterday. Suddenly, her headache made a hell of a lot more sense.

"First morning I met Reese, she fell cleaning the window, and the fucking mirror crashed down around her. Sliced open her hand. I had to take her to get stitches. I forgot about that damn thing. I figured Nan wouldn't even notice." But I knew she had. Because Rush was calling me. If she'd been cruel to Reese, I'd be paying her a visit, and it wouldn't be one she fucking wanted.

"She probably wouldn't have. Except Reese told her about it and promised to pay her back," Rush said, still sounding annoyed by something.

"Shit! I should've replaced the damn thing. I just got . . . busy with stuff and forgot."

"Yeah, you should have. She brought Nan a check for two thousand four hundred dollars today after Nan had her fired from the agency. My guess is she lost all her jobs. And she's fucking broke. I was going to take the check away from Nan, but I was afraid she'd press charges against Reese or some stupid shit like that. I'm thinking Reese might need a little help right now."

"Two thousand? What the hell! How much does Nan want for the damn mirror?"

She was the meanest, most vindictive bitch I had ever met. When she'd offered to help Harlow with a blood transfusion after Lila Kate's birth, I thought for a moment that she'd found a heart. But apparently not.

"She's claiming it cost five grand and came from Paris. I'm calling bullshit on that, but she's determined to get her money for it. I figured I would stop this if you didn't. I just know that if it was Blaire being fucked with, I'd want to be the one righting the wrong. Not someone else."

"I'll be there by morning. Don't let Nan get near Reese again. I'm coming to settle this shit and bring Reese back with me. I can't get things done, because my mind's always on her. I want her here."

"Nan will stay away for now. I wasn't happy, and she knows I'm pissed. I also informed her that she'd just fucked with your girlfriend. She didn't take that info well. I believe when I left, she was ranting about 'not believing this fucking shit.'" Rush chuckled. But my mind was already on to the next thing. I had plans to make and a girl to persuade to move to Texas with me.

After ending the call with Rush, I started packing and made phone calls to my stepdad and Major. I told them there was some stuff I needed to handle out of town and left them with the list of things I needed help with while I was gone.

Then I headed to the airport and took the first flight out.

⌗

Not going directly to Reese was hard. But I was going to deal with my "dear sister" first. The plane touched down close to midnight. I had arranged for Rush to send the truck I usually borrowed when I was in town to the airport.

It was a little after two in the morning when I pulled up to Nan's gate after plugging the code into the security box. Lights were still on in the house. She was still awake. Good. I wouldn't have to wake her up.

I didn't bother knocking, I just used the code and went on in. I could hear the television and laughter in the media room. I walked through the foyer and headed straight for the noise.

Nan was on the sofa with a glass of wine in her hand, telling another girl who sat across from her about something that was apparently hilarious. I didn't see Nan as the funny type. Or a good storyteller.

Her eyes caught mine, and she jolted right before the anger flashed in her eyes. "You can't barge into my house like this, Mase. I'm calling the cops," she snapped.

"Please, do. I'll just call our father and let him deal with them, since this is his house. He's let me know more than once that I'm welcome to use it whenever I want to."

Just like I knew they would, my words stopped her cold. She hated any reason to involve Kiro in her life. And she also knew I was right. This wasn't her house. She didn't pay for it or one damn thing in it. I found out that last bit when I called Kiro while waiting for my flight. He paid for the house to come furnished. That mirror wasn't something she'd even bought. *Bitch.*

Mean bitch.

"I can't believe you're here because of her. She was my housecleaner, Mase. Surely you can do better than that. It's kind of low for Kiro's son. Does Daddy Dearest know you were banging the help while you were here?" There was a bitterness to Nan that I had never seen in anyone her age before. It ate her up. Made her cruel and heartless. And so fucking shallow.

"This is your only warning, little sister. You say one more negative word about Reese, and I'll make sure you regret it for years. Do you understand me? Because I swear to God, I am dead serious."

Her lip drew up in a snarl, and she turned to look at her friend. "I'm sorry about this, Laney. I'm sure he'll be gone once he's done bitching."

I barely glanced at the redhead, but I had seen enough to know she was more interested in me being here than Nan was. "I called Kiro. This place was bought furnished. That damn mirror didn't cost five grand. Furthermore, I did some more research. Reese fell and sliced her hand open in your house on your things while working. She then got fired for it. I'm her witness, because I was here, and I was the one who rushed her to the hospital to get it stitched up. There's a medical record of the stitches. Way I see it, Reese needs a lawyer, 'cause she's got one hell of a case. This whole situation is a fucking lawsuit just waiting to happen. She was hurt on the job and then fired over it. She can sue the cleaning agency, and she can fucking sue you. Wouldn't that make the headlines?"

Nan's eyes went wide, and I enjoyed every damn minute of it as my words sank in.

"I'm even going to suggest that she sue you for the money she's already given you, plus a million dollars for pain and suffering. You are Kiro Manning's daughter, after all. She might as well go for a lot. You can afford it."

Nan let out a laugh that sounded forced. "She can't afford a damn lawyer. That's not going to happen."

"She won't have to pay for one. I've already called mine."

Nan slammed her wineglass down and stood up. "Really, Mase? You, too? The whole damn family hates me. Now you're going to take sides with some girl you're fucking?"

I took a step toward her, reminding myself that I didn't hit women. But dammit, that was hard. I wanted to wring her neck. "Don't. Ever. Call. Reese. That. Again. She's more than you could ever imagine. She doesn't even know I'm here, because she didn't tell me about this bullshit with you. Rush did." I let that sink in. Then I added one more thing. "You bring the hate on yourself, Nan. Stop being a bitch."

I had said what I came to say. Turning, I headed for the door.

"Rush called you?" Her voice sounded smaller. Even the brother she adored, who loved her when no one else did, was done with her bullshit. She was getting that, finally.

"Yeah. He did. He hates to see Reese suffer at your evil hands, too," I said, glancing back at her.

She didn't look so angry anymore. Crestfallen was a better description. It was a shame there wasn't one small piece of me that cared. We shared a father, but I hated this woman. Not just for what she had done to Reese but for how she had treated Harlow when she first came to Rosemary Beach, too. I didn't hate easily, but Nan made sure to bring that emotion out in people.

"Wait. Here, take the damn check. I don't want any more money. But I don't want to see her again, either. She isn't getting her job back."

I turned and took the check from her outstretched hand. She'd just left all of Reese's life savings lying there on her coffee table under a bowl of fruit, as if it were a napkin.

Tucking it safely into my pocket, I gave Nan one last pitying look. "I hope you figure out one day that piss and vinegar ain't attractive. After a while, you can turn everyone away from you for good. Snap out of whatever this shit is that controls your head, and change. Because you've lost everyone else already. Don't lose Rush, too."

The pain that sliced through her expression was enough. I left.

I was ready to go take care of my girl.

Reese

A ringing in the distance interrupted my dreams, and I turned in circles to look for the source. I saw nothing but the clouds around me. The ringing stopped, but then it started up again. Frustrated, I stomped my feet, but then it dawned on me. This was a dream.

My eyes snapped open, and the ringing was my cell phone. Rubbing my eyes, I sat up and looked for it, still a little disoriented. The sun hadn't risen, and it was still very dark outside. It had taken me forever to fall asleep.

My phone continued to ring until, finally, I saw the screen glowing in the darkness. I climbed out of bed and picked it up from where it had fallen to the floor. Cowboy boots. Mase.

"Hello," I said in a hoarse whisper.

"You have someone at your door. Could you open it so both of you can crawl back into bed and go to sleep?" he said in his deep, sexy drawl on the other end of the line.

I frowned, and then I heard the knock. It took me a few seconds to register that Mase was at my door. I dropped my phone onto the bed and took off running to open the door. Why was he here? His phone call earlier tonight had been so short it had worried me. He hadn't even asked me to read to him.

This was why. He was coming to see me.

I threw open the door, and he stepped into the apartment, looking as perfect as always. It was then that I realized my hair was probably sticking up everywhere. I hadn't even checked myself in the mirror.

But he was here. I just didn't care about anything else.

"Sorry I woke you up, but I didn't want to sleep in the truck all night when I could crawl into bed and sleep with you in my arms."

Swoon. This man and his words.

I grinned. I was so happy to see him I couldn't help it. I knew I had the silly grin on my face that I got when I was giddy. But having Mase here made me giddy. I hadn't expected to see him again so soon, and after the week I'd had so far, I needed this.

Just being with him fixed everything.

He closed the distance between us and ran his hand over my hair with an amused smirk on his lips. "I like this. Seeing you like this."

I wanted to melt into him. "You're here," was all I could say.

He nodded. "I am. We can talk about it tomorrow. Let's get you back into bed."

He was coming with me. This was . . . oh, crap. I was dreaming. I would have bet this was a dream. It was the only thing that made sense. I didn't want this to be a dream. I wanted him to be here, dammit.

"Pinch me," I told him, as his hand slipped to my lower back.

He frowned. "Why would I do that?"

"To prove I'm not dreaming," I explained.

His deep chuckle made me tingle all over. "How about I do this instead?" he said, just before his mouth covered mine.

I had started to open for him when he gently bit my bottom lip with a small snap that caused me to jump. "See, baby? You're awake," he said, sliding his hand down over my bottom and squeezing it once before moving it back up to my lower back.

I wanted more of that, but he was once again leading me back to the bedroom.

"Why are you here?" I asked, when he straightened the messy covers and pulled them back for me. I crawled in obediently.

"Because I needed to see you," he said simply.

I watched him take off his boots and unbutton his flannel shirt and throw it onto the chair. He was wearing an undershirt that fit so snugly I could make out every beautiful line of definition on his chest and back. When he turned to get into bed beside me, I pulled the covers back for him. I didn't want him to think he still had to sleep on the top. He still had on his jeans. Those couldn't be comfortable.

"You can take off your jeans. You'll sleep better," I told him, before he sank down on the bed beside me.

He paused for only a moment and then started unbuttoning his jeans. I felt his gaze on me as he did it, but I was too riveted to look at his face. His big hands quickly unzipped the jeans, and they slipped down his thick, muscular thighs. I had to gulp in air. I'd forgotten to breathe.

"You sure you're OK with this? I can sleep in my jeans, baby."

He was worried that I was freaking out over him being

in his underwear. Well, I was freaking out but for a differ-ent reason. Mase Manning really made white boxer briefs look yummy. I had been panicked after breaking that mirror, so enjoying that first glimpse hadn't been on my agenda that day. But right now . . .

"I'm good. I mean, you're good. I mean, I'm fine, and . . . oh, just get into bed," I rambled.

Mase smirked this time. Then he slid in beside me, but he was careful not to touch me. I had reacted so badly to mak-ing out and touching last time that he was now gun-shy. But I wasn't sure I had the nerve to make a move on him or ask him to do anything. The idea of it being all on me was stressful.

It didn't matter. Not right now. Mase was here tonight, for whatever reason. I curled up to his side, and he pulled me in closer, but he didn't do anything else. Glancing up at him, I could see his long eyelashes fanning his cheekbones. He'd al-ready closed his eyes. Smiling contentedly, I closed mine, too.

✚

The next time I opened my eyes, the sun was filtering in through the blinds, and Mase was now on his side, with me wrapped up in his arms. I tilted my head back to see if he was awake. His eyes were still closed, but his arms tightened around me as a small smile tugged on his lips.

"You awake?" he asked groggily, then slowly opened his eyes and met my gaze.

"Yes," I replied, feeling entirely too high on life for a girl without a job or money.

"Hmm . . . you want to tell me all about your week now or over coffee and waffles?"

Grinning, I pressed a kiss to his arm. "Is that your way of asking me to make you waffles?"

He shrugged, grinning like he knew he could get me to do anything. "Maybe."

I kissed his arm again. "You have to let me up in order for me to do that."

His head lowered, and he ran his lips gently over my forehead. "But you feel so good all snuggled up soft in my arms."

I would agree that this was my favorite spot ever. On earth.

"Why don't you tell me about your week now?" he said in a more serious tone.

He was asking me about my week like he already knew. "I talked to you last night on the phone. You know about my week," I said, testing him.

"No . . . I only know what you've told me. I want the whole story. Nothing left out." The teasing in his voice was gone now. He knew. That was why he was here.

"Who told you?" I asked, moving back, or at least trying to. His hold on me didn't loosen.

"You should have," was his reply.

"It wasn't your problem."

That got his attention. His eyes snapped open wide, and he moved fast. I thought for a second that he was getting up, but he flipped me on my back and put one hand on each side of my head and hovered over me. "Anything that affects you is my problem. You're mine. Even if I didn't know what happened that day. Even if Nan wasn't my sister. This would be my problem, because it hurts you. It causes you pain." His voice softened on that last sentence. He lowered his body, but he didn't press against me. He nuzzled my neck for a moment, and my entire body came to life. A sensation of warmth spread through me. "When you hurt, it rips me apart. When you're happy, I feel like I own the fucking world."

This man was too much. "You have a ranch to run and a life in Texas. I didn't want to bother you with this."

Mase sighed and kissed my jaw before moving back to look down at me. "I have a ranch to run, and it's in Texas. But you trump all that. If you need me, you come first."

I love you was right there on the tip of my tongue. I wanted him to know. But he wasn't saying those words to me. I was afraid he would think I was naive and confused about what we were doing. So I kept them to myself. But I screamed them in my head and my soul. I loved this man.

"Your check is in the pocket of my jeans. Nan gave that back to me last night. You don't owe her anything. She didn't buy that mirror. Kiro bought the house furnished. It's all his, and he doesn't give a shit about that mirror."

I just stared up at him. I didn't know what to say to that. I had seen the fury on Nan's face. I wasn't so sure she would agree to this. When Mase left, the cops were likely to show up and arrest me. That money I gave her was my proof that I intended to pay her back.

"I need her to have that money, Mase."

He shook his head. "It's handled. She won't bother you again."

When he was gone, she would. "You can't protect me from everything."

"I can protect you from my sister. And fuck yes, I can protect you from everything. Send that shit my way. I'll take it out." He was smiling, but I could see the seriousness in his eyes.

"Mase," I started, but he put his finger over my lips.

"I got this. I handled it. She's afraid of a lawsuit from you. You were hurt at her house on the job, then fired over it. She will not contact you again. Hell, she probably won't breathe the same air you do for a while. I was very thorough in my descriptions of what I would do if she fucked with you any more."

"I wouldn't sue her because I fell and broke a mirror."

"She doesn't know that, baby. And that's all that matters." He rolled off me and got up. I was blessed with a view of his butt in those white briefs. God bless America and Mase Manning's ass.

"You gonna get that sweet tail up and make me some waffles? Because, baby, if you keep looking at me like I'm the meal, I may be tempted to crawl back into that bed and see exactly what you had in mind."

I would love for him to crawl back into bed and do things with me. To me. But I didn't want to have to ask him to do stuff. I wasn't sure how I was going to do that. I knew why he wanted me to, but still . . . the idea was so embarrassing.

How did one ask a man to touch her vagina?

Cringing at that thought, I stood up and flashed a smile at him. "I'm going to make you some waffles. Put on your jeans so I'm not distracted."

Mase laughed as I hurried to the bathroom to brush my hair and teeth.

Then I went and made my guy some breakfast, while he stood on the other side of the bar and watched me.

Mase

If she bent over one more time and flashed that freckle at me, I was going to lose my mind. I had eaten my waffles and made it through her stirring the batter with no bra on under that tank top. That had been one hell of a pretty sight. But now she was cleaning up the kitchen, and she kept bending over.

I had offered to clean up, but she had pushed me out of the tiny corner and said she'd do it faster since she knew where everything was. So now I was being given a view of her ass and that freckle. My freckle.

I loved that freckle.

Shit, I was horny. She had me so wound up, and I was trying so hard to be good. But I knew how that ass felt in my hands and those sweet nipples tightened under my tongue.

Groaning, I turned away from the prettiest sight I'd ever seen and walked over to sit on the sofa.

I sank down and had to adjust my damn dick. My jeans were suddenly too tight, and the zipper was going to leave a mark on it if I didn't get myself under control. I needed to think about something other than Reese's body.

First boner killer I could think of: my mother. She would want to know where I'd gone. I needed to call her and explain.

I had only called my stepdad. I hadn't explained myself to her. Which meant she was going to ask me a lot of questions. I was ready to tell her about Reese. I wanted to talk about her. My mom was probably the one person who would want to listen to me talk about her.

"You OK?" Reese's voice broke into my thoughts, and I turned to see her walking my way. Those long legs and . . . fuck, those tits were jiggling. She needed a bra. I needed her to wear a bra. The boner I'd deflated was back with a vengeance. Fuck me.

"I'm good," I assured her, and she came and sank down beside me, pulling her legs back and curling into my side. Soft flesh pressed against me, and I was throbbing. The cinnamon sweet smell met my nose, and I stretched out my legs in hopes of giving myself some more room in these jeans.

"You don't look good. You're grimacing," she said, reaching up and cupping my face. So damn sweet.

"I'm trying to be good, baby. But looking at you makes it hard," I admitted.

"Oh," she said softly. Almost a whisper. Then her eyes dropped to my lap, and she sucked in a breath.

There was no hiding the fact I was hard as a rock. I hadn't dealt with this kind of shit since high school. I didn't get boners anymore unless I was about to get some. One look at Reese, though, and my cock stood at attention.

"It looks like it's tight in there," she said, still whispering as if someone other than me could hear her.

"It is."

She took another quick breath, then reached down to touch my leg. I was real close to begging her to touch me. My brain was losing blood by the second, and it was all headed south. "Will you take it out and let me . . . I mean, can I touch it?"

Hell, yes!

My hands shot to my fly and got it undone in record time, then I tugged my jeans down my hips enough so that my cock sprang free. She was watching me so intently I swear I was about to explode from her just looking at it.

Her fingertips slowly traced the hard ridge through my briefs. I hadn't pulled those down. I wasn't sure she was ready to actually see it.

"Can you take it out?" she asked, her eyes looking up at me, then dropping back to my lap.

This girl was asking me like I would tell her no. My dick had decided more than a month ago that it only wanted to perform for her. She owned it as much as she owned me.

I paused and watched her face to make sure she was ready for this before pulling my briefs back and letting her see what it was she was asking for. I really did not want her jumping up and running off to splash water on her face from the sight of my cock. The idea of scaring her this way would wreck me.

Her hand moved as if in slow motion until one fingertip ran down the hard swollen head and the veins along the length. I couldn't breathe. Oxygen refused to go into my lungs. "Tell me how to touch it," she said, running a finger back up toward the head.

She wanted me to fucking talk now? "Wrap—" I said, then gasped in some air. "Wrap your hand around it, and slide it up and down."

She did exactly as I said, and stars filled my vision. I had to blink several times to clear it. I stared down at her small hand around my dick, and I leaked fucking precome. She paused. Her eyes lifted to mine.

"You like this?" she asked, her breathing heavy. This was exciting her. Fuck, her nipples were hard and poking through that thin top.

"You have no idea," I replied tightly.

She tightened her grasp when she slid up, and her eyes widened as the clear fluid appeared at the tip.

"Fuuuck," I groaned, and laid my head back on the sofa. I was in some form of nirvana, and I didn't want to come out of it.

"Too tight?" she asked, innocently.

"God, baby, no. So good," I panted.

Her grip stayed tight, and she began moving up and down my dick with more vigor. My mouth fell open once, and I grabbed the arm of the sofa to hold on.

"Was that come, or will you . . . come more?" she asked as the precome coated my dick under her grasp. She hadn't recoiled, but instead, she'd used it for lubrication.

"You keep this up, and I'm going to . . . explode."

The little minx grinned. She was enjoying herself. Fuck me, but that was almost too much. I wanted to hold back and enjoy this longer. I wasn't going to scare the hell out of her and come all over her hand. But making her let go so I could finish under my own hand didn't sound appealing.

I turned my head to look at her, and that was the mistake. She had her bottom lip pulled between her teeth, and with each move of her hand, her tits bounced. I was done.

"I'm gonna come," I said, taking her hand off me.

"Wait, no," she said, reaching for me again.

"Baby, I'm gonna—"

The upward tug and the smell of her hit me at once. I cried out her name as I did exactly as I'd warned her. She kept moving her hand on me, and I kept on fucking coming. Falling back against the sofa, I think I might have whimpered. I wasn't sure anymore. My brain was fuzzy, and my body was humming with a pleasure so intense I wasn't sure I'd walk again.

Then her hand stopped moving, and I sucked in a deep breath.

"Holy shit, that was . . . incredible," I said, staring down at her small hand covered in my release.

Just the sight of it had my dick stirring to life again. Dammit, she was turning me into an animal. I'd just had the best orgasm of my life from her hand.

"Let me clean you up," I said, tugging up my underwear and standing to pull my jeans up on my hips. "I'll get a washcloth." I started, but she stood up, smiling.

"I'll go wash it off," she assured me. Then she shoved me back down. "You seem like you need a moment."

My girl had jokes. I laughed, and she threw a glance back and winked at me. She motherfucking *winked* at me.

Reese

I washed my hands under the warm water and looked at the silly smile on my face. I had done that. I had made Mase groan and cry out and even grab the sofa like his life depended on it until he got off. Me. I did it. And not one time had I gone to that dark place. I had been all wrapped up in watching Mase and knowing I was the one giving him that pleasure. It was a high. I had gotten some crazy high from it.

Then the way he'd looked at me, in awe, like I was some wonderful gift. He always made me feel special, but in that moment, I felt like a goddess. His goddess.

"You are entirely too pleased with yourself," his deep voice said, and I watched through the mirror as he walked up behind me. He had a lazy, satisfied grin on his face, and I had put it there. I *was* pleased with myself.

"I am," I admitted.

He pulled my hair back away from my neck and pressed a kiss there. "Mmm-hmm, it's cute and sexy," he said in a whisper. "But it's also fucking hot."

I felt goose bumps cover my skin when his tongue darted out and licked my neck. "I just have one small problem with it," he said, then nipped at my ear.

"Yeah?"

His hand pressed against my stomach and pulled me back against him. "Yeah. I do. You got to see me come all over your hand. Now I want to see you come all over mine," he said, as his fingers teased the waistline of my shorts.

We had tried that before. I'd panicked. I didn't want to mess this morning up. "What if I'm not ready?" I asked, unable to deny how the way his fingertips slipped into the top of my bottoms made me tremble with excitement.

He paused a moment, and then his mouth trailed kisses back down my neck and across my shoulder. "I thought about that. I've been thinking about it. I need to keep you with me when I touch you. So I want to try it again, but I won't stop talking to you. I will reassure you the whole time and make sure you know it's me. Can we try?"

My breasts were aching, but the space between my legs felt like it was on fire. I wanted this. My body wanted it. And I loved Mase. He wanted this. "OK," I replied.

"Thank fuck," he growled. He picked me up like a child and carried me to the bed and lay down beside me. "You smell so good. When I'm back home, I lie in my bed at night, and I can smell a hint of you. It teases me. I want you there. With me," he whispered in my ear, as he slowly began easing his hand inside my shorts. I didn't have on panties underneath, and he was about to find that out.

When he slid down far enough to realize it, he stopped. "Baby, you aren't wearing panties," he said in a deep voice.

I turned my head so I could see him.

His eyes looked much like they did when I was touching him. This excited him *that* much. The wetness between my legs got worse, and I was embarrassed for him to discover how turned-on I was.

"Open your legs. Please, for me. Let me touch you. I want to see you come for me. Feel your wetness on my hand. Can you give me that, Reese? I want it so bad."

I swallowed nervously. "I'm wet now," I said, feeling mortified at even having to say it.

His eyes flashed something so intense it made my heart skip a beat. His fingers slid down over my mound and into the folds below. The needy ache I'd had down there all morning was now a throb, and I had to grab his arm to keep from shooting off the bed.

"Oh, fuck," he said in a low groan, and he buried his head in my neck. "Sweetest pussy in the world is soaking wet for me."

He was happy about it. I would have breathed a sigh of relief, but his fingers began to move, and all I could do was make noises and hold on to his arm and a fistful of the sheet.

"That's all me. My hand between your legs. My fingers touching your little pussy. Me, baby. Me. It's all mine. I'll always take care of you. Nothing or no one will hurt you." His voice was low and at my ear. I was shivering and clinging to him.

He wanted to keep me in the moment with him, and he was doing a wonderful job. I wasn't sure I could be anywhere else.

"When you're ready, I'm going to put my mouth right here," he said, as he ran his finger over my most sensitive spot. "I'm going to lick this button until you scream and claw at my back while you come on my face. You'll love it. I swear you will. You will hold my head there and beg me not to stop. Because it will be me."

The building feeling inside of me was growing, and I knew

what this was. I'd once brought myself to release before things . . . happened. I had played fantasies in my head with boys at school while in bed at night. But this was something stronger. It was similar, but it was bigger. I wanted it. I wanted it with Mase.

"That's it, baby. Let me have your pleasure. Give it to me. I want to see you fall apart for me. I want to see my girl feel good in my arms. You're so beautiful."

With those words, I broke apart, screaming his name as my body shook and he held me tight. His hand stayed on me, cupping me and riding through the waves of ecstasy with me. I was chanting his name. I heard it in the distance.

He was calling me baby and telling me I was incredible.

I didn't want to come back. This trip was one I could live on.

But eventually, it eased, and I slowly descended back to earth. Mase's arms were still around me, holding me close, and his hand remained on me. His breathing was hard, and his eyes were dark and heated as he stared down at me. "God, you're gorgeous," he breathed, as I blinked and finally focused on him.

I couldn't talk just yet. That hadn't been at all what I'd experienced in my bed when I was younger. My fingers did not make me do that. Was that even healthy? It was so good it had to be dangerous. And I wanted to do it again. Now.

"I don't want to move my hand. It's coated with you, and I want to keep it that way," he said, moving his head to press a kiss to my nose. "That was the most erotic thing I've ever seen. I swear to God, you've got me so wrapped around you I can't see straight. I'd stay in this bed and make you come over and over if you'd let me."

I would let him. I was liking that idea. A lot.

Mase

I could die a happy man. I felt sorry for the other men in the world, because they'd never know what Reese looked like when she came. I did. She was mine. The urge to pound on my chest was strong. I fought it off. But God, I wanted to.

Reese came out of the bedroom dressed in blue jeans shorts and a pale yellow blouse that tied at the waist. She looked young and fresh. I wanted to take her back to bed and sink into all of it. Watch her get naughty and ride my hand like her life depended on it.

But she'd given me enough today. I wasn't pushing her again. Not when we'd been so successful this morning. My talking to her and keeping her with me the whole time had not only worked, but it had excited her more. The more I talked, the more turned-on she got.

It was enough for now.

"When do you have to leave?" she asked, breaking into my thoughts and reminding me that I had to leave her.

"I wanted to talk to you about that," I said, wondering how to ask her to move in with me several states away. It sounded a little crazy, but honestly, I didn't care. She was my one.

Her brow puckered up, and she tilted her head as if waiting for me.

"I want you to move to . . . Texas . . . with me . . . into . . . my house."

That hadn't been smooth at all.

The way her jaw dropped open and her eyes turned into saucers proved I had gone about this all wrong. *Shit.*

"Wh-what?" she sputtered.

I ran my hands over my face and bit back a growl of frustration. She made me just say shit. I got so worked up around her I couldn't think straight. I just blurted things out. I had never wanted anything as badly as I wanted this woman in my bed every night for the rest of my life.

"You don't have a job except for your gig at Harlow's, and you don't have family here. There's no reason to stay. I can get another reading teacher to work with you in Fort Worth. That would be the only thing holding you here. I want you with me, Reese. I hate not having you close."

Those expressive eyes of hers gave her away. She liked the idea, but it also scared her. We were new. Our friendship was almost two months old now, but as a couple, we were new.

"You want me there . . . with you," she said, sounding like she was lost in a daze.

"Yes," I replied firmly.

She fisted a section of her hair and looked around the room nervously. Then she began walking back and forth in a little circle. Almost as if she was pacing.

I waited. She was thinking, and I wanted her to think about this hard. Then I wanted her to say yes and pack her bags.

"You don't . . . there's so much. I need time. We need time. I'm settled here, and I do have friends. I have Jimmy. I have a place that is mine. You can't . . . we can't just move in together like this. I hate when you leave, too, but . . . but Mase." She stopped walking and dropped her hands to her sides as if she was carrying the world on her shoulders. "There is so much you don't know. And I'm not ready to tell you. So much that is inside me. It's dark, and it's . . . not a place I want to take you. But I need time. We need time. Like this. When you come into town, we can spend time together. And our nightly talks and my reading to you. And I like Dr. Munroe. He's helping me, and I'm comfortable with him. I can't just go with you because I want to be near you."

Arguing with her was my knee-jerk reaction. I was good at debate. I could come up with a reason that all that didn't matter.

What stopped me was the pleading look in her eyes. She didn't want me to argue. She wanted me to let this go.

I would. For her. For now.

"OK. Then know that when you're ready, I will be, too," I finally said.

She let out a heavy sigh, then smiled weakly at me. "Thank you for wanting me."

Words I would take back to Texas with me, that I would carry like an ache in my chest every time I thought of them.

My girl should never have to thank anyone for wanting her. Somewhere in her mind, she thought she wasn't worthy. That was what hurt the most.

⊞

Standing at her door after taking her to lunch and kissing her for more than an hour, I knew I had to leave her. Again. My world back home was calling. I had to go handle the ranch and the life I'd made for myself.

I held her tightly one more time and whispered in her ear. "Be safe. Take care of yourself. And miss me when I'm gone."

Reese

I took the spoon Jimmy handed me and dove into the caramel swirl ice cream with a vengeance. I needed depression food. I'd been in the dumps since Mase had left that morning. I could have gone with him. He'd asked me to.

If I had said yes, I would have lost him much sooner. He hadn't been with me long enough to really know me. He'd only gotten small doses of me. What about when the memories leaked through and I stood under the hot water of the shower screaming and scrubbing myself? He hadn't seen that. He would think I was crazy. Because I was sure I was.

Sometimes the past broke through, and when it did, I went a little crazy.

I kept all that from him. He knew what was on the surface, and not even all of that. He knew just enough. My past had marked me.

It had ruined my ability to be close to anyone.

Except Mase. I was letting him in. Today proved just how much.

"You wanna talk about it? Or just eat it out?" Jimmy asked with a pinched frown.

"Don't want to talk about it," I replied, and stuffed my mouth full of ice cream.

"The man came from Texas on a Tuesday night to get your money back from the wicked witch and make sure you were OK before heading back home the next day to work. Seems to me like you should be all smiles and giggles. Not pissy and trying to eat your way through this whole pint of ice cream."

I wasn't telling Jimmy. If I did, I'd have to tell him more, and I wasn't letting my past in. Not tonight. "I just hate it when he leaves," I said instead.

"Mmm-hmm, girl, so does the rest of the world. He's something to look at," Jimmy agreed.

That got a laugh out of me that died almost instantly. The girls in Fort Worth didn't have to see him leave. He was there. With them. They could see him and talk to him. He didn't have to fly over state borders to fix their problems.

"Wherever your head just went, bring it back, please," Jimmy said, pointing his spoon at me. "The man flew his ass over here for you last night. He ain't giving anyone else nothing. Hell, I doubt he even smiles in Texas. He's smiling too much for you. He's gotta rest his sexy mouth sometime."

I laughed. Loudly.

Jimmy sat back and smirked. He was pleased with himself.

The sound of my phone ringing had him standing up and saluting me. "That's your piece of hot Texas ass now. I'll talk to you tomorrow."

I glanced down at the phone, expecting to see cowboy boots, but it was an unknown caller. I didn't let Jimmy know.

"'Bye, Jimmy. And thanks," I called out.

He blew me a kiss and closed the door behind him.

I waited a moment until he was away from the door before answering.

"Hello."

"You think you have him, but you don't. He was fucking me before you, and he'll be fucking me after you."

I held the phone in my hand long after the woman had ended the call.

An hour later, Mase called to tell me he was home safe but he was exhausted. He'd call me tomorrow.

❖

The next morning, I refused to think about the strange phone call. It could have been a wrong number. She never said Mase's name. I shoved it aside and finally called Blaire Finlay to set up a meeting with her for the next week about cleaning her house. Then I went to the store and paid my bills for the week.

I came back to the apartment and cleaned it from top to bottom. By the time I had to meet with Dr. Munroe, I was better. I had gotten myself together, and I knew that when I called Mase that night, all would be well.

I was just missing him.

That was all this was.

Mase

I undressed and lay back on the bed while listening to Reese read me her newest book. She seemed off tonight or nervous. I wasn't sure which. I had to help her several times. Once she reached the end of chapter two, I was going to let her stop. This book was more difficult, and she seemed tired.

"Do you want me to keep going?" she asked.

"That's good. You're doing so much better, baby. I'm so proud of you." And I was. She was reading on a fourth-grade level already. Dr. Munroe said it was because she had tried hard to learn in school, and she had learned. She just hadn't been shown how to deal with her disability. Now that she was working with it, she was picking up quickly and utilizing things she'd already been taught.

"My writing isn't the best, but I wrote a letter today. It wasn't a real one. I was supposed to write a fake one to someone thanking them for a gift. I only messed up two words. Dr. Munroe was pleased." The pride in her voice made my chest tighten. I loved knowing that she was proud of her accomplishments. She should be.

"I'm waiting for you to write me a letter," I told her. I could keep it tucked in my pocket all day and pull it out when I needed my Reese fix.

She laughed softly. "Not ready for that yet. Let me get better at it. I don't want Dr. Munroe correcting a letter I wrote to you. So it will have to come to you unedited."

Nothing she gave me could be less than perfect. Because it would be her. What she wrote. If she mixed up every letter and every word, then that was the way they were fucking meant to be. Because she would have written them for me.

"Don't care how many mistakes are in it, Reese. It would be from you. That's all that matters," I told her.

She made a soft little sigh. "You say the sweetest things."

I could say even sweeter things if she'd let me. I was tempted to try. Swear to God, I could still smell her on my hand. I'd put those fingers up to my nose and inhaled all damn day.

"What are you wearing, Reese?" I asked.

"Your T-shirt, just like I'm supposed to," she replied. I could hear the amusement in her voice.

"Go lie down on your bed for me." I was testing her. I'd stop if she balked even once.

"OK," she breathed. "I'm on my bed."

Fuck. Yes. She was playing along.

"You lying down?" I wanted her on her back with her legs open for me.

"Yes." Her response was quick and anxious-sounding. She knew what I was wanting.

"Will you let those pretty legs fall open for me, baby?" I waited, not knowing if she'd go this far.

After only a few seconds, she replied. "Yes."

I pulled my hardening cock out of my briefs and wrapped

my hand around it. The image of Reese lying back on her bed in my shirt with her legs open for me had me ready to get back on the damn plane.

"You know what I want you to do, don't you?"

"Yeah," she whispered.

"Will you? Can I hear you pleasure yourself?"

She was breathing heavily. "Will you?"

"Will I what, baby?"

"Will you do it, too?"

Grinning, I stroked my length. "Already doing it. The fact that you're on your bed with those legs open wearing my shirt has me so damn turned-on I'm aching."

"Oh," she said, then let out a soft moan.

Fuck . . . me . . . she was doing it. "Where're your fingers?"

"On my . . . down there," she replied.

Oh, yeah. I closed my eyes and let her voice and the image of what she was doing take over my thoughts. "Are you wet for me?"

"Yeaaah," she said, with a hitch in her breathing.

"Play with it easy for me. Make my sweet pussy feel good. I'm not there to take care of it. I need you to, and let me hear you. I wanna hear those sounds you make."

"Ahhh!" she cried out. She loved my words.

"Rub that hard, swollen clit. I want to kiss it. So bad . . . Run my tongue along the tender spots and then suck that hot button into my mouth until you pull my hair and scream my name."

"Ohhhh, God," she moaned.

"That's it. Think about my head between those legs. All open for me. I can lick and lap up all that sweetness. Just me.

Right there with you. Just us, baby. Your hands fisted in my hair and my hands . . . *my* hands on your creamy smooth thighs, holding you open. Breathing you in."

"Mase! Oh . . . aaaaah!"

Her release gave me my own. I listened as she rode it out and wished to God I was there to see it.

Reese

Over the next week, I didn't just read to Mase at night. We ended our evenings doing other things . . .

Smiling at my secret, I spent extra time brushing my hair. I had cleaned Harlow's house twice and met with Blaire Finlay. She was going to need someone three days a week. I had to talk to Harlow about working in her two days and Blaire's three days to meet everyone's needs. Blaire's current housecleaner hadn't retired yet, so there was time to figure it out. She had two more weeks.

Jimmy had found out earlier in the week that today was my birthday. He'd decided he was taking me out. I hadn't done anything more than celebrate all alone most of my life. I remembered having a cake once when I was seven. My mother had made one and invited the neighborhood children over. I'd thought she had done it for me, and for a little while, I had felt so special.

Then, later that day, I had found her in the bathroom on her knees in front of one of the dads at the party. He had been saying things I didn't want to remember while she gripped his thighs and gave him a blow job. That man lived across the street with his wife and two kids.

I had realized that not only was something wrong with what my mother was doing, but she had thrown this party to get close to that man. Not to me. It was my first and last birthday cake.

Tonight I would make a new memory. Jimmy wanted us to go dancing and eat cake. So we were going to do just that. I would celebrate turning twenty-three with someone who cared about me.

Stepping back and looking into the mirror, I felt like I was pretty. The dress I had on was a soft orange and reminded me of a sunset. It was strapless and belted at my waist with a brown woven belt that fell to mid-thigh. I had slipped on the cowboy boots I'd bought to please Mase. He hadn't seen them yet, but I used some of my savings to buy them. They were on sale for half-price, so I had only spent a little too much on them instead of a lot.

The knock on the door was followed by an "Open up, birthday girl!"

I smiled and went to let Jimmy inside.

He let out a low whistle and twirled his finger in the air for me to spin around. "I'm gonna have to act straight tonight to keep the men off you. Damn, woman, you clean up fine."

Laughing, I grabbed the small clutch I'd bought last year at a thrift store but never had a chance to use. It was metallic gold but simple, with a wristlet strap. "Let's go dance," I told him, as he took my hand and tucked it into the crook of his arm.

"I got moves, girl. You just wait."

I had no doubt he did.

⌗

We headed into town instead of out of it, but I knew there was nowhere to dance in Rosemary Beach. Frowning, I glanced over at Jimmy, who was singing "Born in the U.S.A." and tapping his steering wheel like it was drums.

"Where are we dancing?" I asked.

"Ah, some place called FloraBama," he replied, flashing me a smile that was too big. Something was off.

"But we aren't headed out of town," I pointed out.

He nodded in agreement. "Yeah. Gotta drop something off first at the club."

Well, that made sense. I sat back and watched the small town pass by as we turned into the back entrance of the club where the workers parked. Jimmy drove down toward a shell road that seemed to lead out to the water.

Was he dropping something off at the beach?

"Here we are," he said, smiling at me as he swung open the door. We had driven down as far as we could go.

"If you'll just walk down this wooden walkway toward that light up ahead," Jimmy said, pointing me toward what looked like the top of a small tent from here. There were palm trees in the way.

"Do you need me to drop it off?" I asked, trying to figure out what he was asking me.

"Yep. Only you can drop off you. Happy birthday, Reese. You look amazing. Now, go follow that path," he said with a wink, then climbed back into his car and drove off. I stood there looking at the path and back to where Jimmy had left.

It was then that it starting sinking in. Jimmy had dropped me off. Me. I turned and headed down the wooden path. Halfway down, I couldn't take it anymore, so I started to run. I knew who was going to be at the end of this path. I knew who he'd dropped me off to. And I wanted to get there.

Once I broke free out of the palm-lined walkway, I saw him.

He was wearing a white button-down shirt with the sleeves rolled up to his elbows and a pair of khaki shorts. He stood inside a white tent illuminated by candlelight, with a three-tiered birthday cake beside him. It was a pretty pale pink and sparkled under the dim lights. Silver balloons filled the tent.

"Happy birthday, Reese," Mase said, smiling.

I let out a startled laugh, then burst into tears and ran for him.

He met me halfway, picked me up in his arms, and buried his face in my neck. "Surprise."

I leaned back and kissed him hard. I didn't know how else to express the emotion that was barreling through me. It was so overwhelming, I felt like I might combust from happiness. He'd done this all for me. A cake and balloons. And most importantly, him.

"How did you know it was my birthday?" I asked, even though the answer was obvious: Jimmy. I had thought about telling Mase but worried he'd think I was asking him to come back again. I didn't want that, so I'd just kept it to myself.

"You should have been the one to tell me, not Jimmy. I never want to miss your birthday. Ever."

I wiped the tears from my face and beamed up at this wonderful man who for some reason wanted to be with me. "You and your words," I said, then kissed him again.

His big, strong hands wrapped around my waist and held me there as we tasted and fed off each other. Having him here with me was the best birthday gift ever. Even without a cake and balloons. He was perfect.

"Come on, you have to blow out the candles, and then I get to feed you cake," he murmured against my lips.

"That's a lot of cake for just us," I said, not even trying to pretend I didn't love that he got me a ginormous cake.

He chuckled. "We'll eat our fill, and you can take some home, and then we can send the leftovers to friends."

I liked that idea. "I may eat too much," I said, looking at the creamy icing and already licking my lips. I would have to walk for days nonstop to burn off these calories.

Mase winked at me. "Good. I like the idea of that hot ass jiggling a little more."

I really needed to fan myself.

He stuck a candle into the top tier and shrugged. "I was going to get twenty-three candles, but Harlow pointed out that the breeze out here was too much. I'd never get them to stay lit. So I went with the one."

He struck a match and hovered over the candle to protect it as he lit it.

"Make a wish, baby."

I couldn't think of anything I didn't have right now . . . except for one thing. But I knew wishes didn't take away the past. They couldn't change what had been done. So instead, I said a small thank you for what I'd been given and blew out the candle.

Mase began slicing a very large piece of cake and took a fork and looked up at me. "Come sit with me." He nodded to the white chaise longue that sat in the corner overlooking the gulf.

He sat down and opened his arms for me to sink into. I was half on top of him when his arms wrapped around me.

"That piece is too big," I said, eyeing the red filling.

"We're sharing," he informed me. "Open up."

I did as he said, and Mase slid the bite into my mouth. The sweet cream of the icing and the raspberry filling were delicious. "Mmm," I said approvingly.

"I like watching you eat. And feeding you," Mase said, as he scooped up another piece of the cake. He started moving it to my mouth, but I shook my head.

"Your piece," I informed him.

"Watching your tongue dart out to lick your lips and listening to you moan is so much better than me eating this cake," he said, and he rubbed some of the icing on my mouth.

I opened my mouth, trying not to laugh as he slipped in another bite.

"Yeah, there comes that tongue," he said, sounding completely fascinated with watching me eat my cake.

I finished chewing and swallowed, then shook my head again. "I need a break in between bites," I told him, laughing while he held another piece up to my face.

"I like your boots," he said, instead of arguing with me. "I want to see you in nothing but those boots."

My purchase had been well worth the cost.

"Please eat more for me. It's so fucking sexy," he begged, running his nose up my neck.

Giggling, I turned and looked at him. "How is me eating sexy?"

Mase smirked, ran a hand down my back, and squeezed my ass. "For several reasons."

"You take a bite," I said, picking up the fork and holding it to his mouth.

He ate obediently, and I kissed the icing off his lips.

"I can see the advantage of me eating it, too, now," he said when I pulled back.

Smiling, I leaned back against his chest and enjoyed the view of the crashing waves in front of me. My legs tangled with his, and he continued to feed me. I let him.

Because I loved this man.

Mase

Reese had given up on the piece of cake, and I'd finally put it down. I had to admit, just seeing her eat it satisfied me, knowing it was a birthday cake that I'd picked out and given to her.

I shifted so she could settle between my legs. I pulled her back against me before giving her the first present.

"Happy birthday," I said, picking up the largest box sitting beside me.

She gasped as she took the box. She glanced back at me before looking at the box again. "You got me a present?" she asked, amazed. "I mean, I thought you were my present, but this . . ."

Smiling, I kissed her temple. "No, this is your party, and I'm your only guest, because I'm selfish and wanted you all to myself. And this is your first present."

"My first?" she asked, and I nodded.

Then she surprised me. She tore into that gift like she was five years old. Watching her open it was more exciting than feeding her cake, and that had been pretty damn exciting.

When she had the lid off the box, she pulled out the baby-blue Michael Kors purse I'd had Blaire help me pick out.

"There's a matching wallet in there, too."

She touched it reverently as if it were made of fine gold instead of leather. "This is expensive, isn't it?"

Not really. It could have been worse. But I'd told Blaire to be practical. Reese needed an everyday purse, not something she would be too nervous to carry.

"It's a nice purse for you to use instead of the backpack," I explained.

She grinned and put it back into the box, then turned to me and kissed me softly on the lips. "Thank you. That's the nicest gift I've ever gotten."

This wasn't over. I reached down and picked up the next present.

"There's more? I thought you were kidding."

"You better believe it."

Again, she tore into it like a little kid, and I found myself wishing I had videotaped this to watch over and over.

She opened the box to find three sets of French silk pajamas. She picked up one of the shorts and held it up and then touched it to her face. Laying it down, she reached for a camisole. The pale pink one with the white lace trim. "These feel so soft," she said in awe.

They should. They were the best.

"I like the idea of you in my T-shirt. But I also know you like your shorts and tank top because they're soft. So I got you some other soft things to sleep in. Because when you're with me, you won't need my T-shirt to wrap around you."

She laid it down in the expensive wrapping and let out a happy sigh. "Those are going to spoil me on pajamas for life."

That was OK. I'd keep her in expensive French silk if she wanted it, for as long as she wanted it.

Again, she kissed me and whispered a thank you against my lips.

I reached for the third box. This one was the smallest. And it was more for me than for her.

"The last one," I told her, as I handed her the rectangular box.

She opened it more carefully, as if she was afraid she would lose whatever was inside.

Inside was a single key nestled in velvet.

"It's the key to my house. When you're ready, you can move in anytime you want."

She picked it up and held it in her hand for several moments and didn't say anything. Finally, she lifted her eyes to meet mine. "One day, when you know all of me, you can give this back to me. But right now, you don't know it all. I can't take this."

She thought her dark past would change how I felt. Nothing she could tell me would change that. I loved her.

But I wouldn't use those words to convince her. She would have to decide this in her own time. I wasn't forcing her. I wanted her in my bed, in my house. I wanted it to be our house. But not until she was ready for that. Not until she wanted me.

Wanted a forever.

Reese

He was acting like me not taking the key wasn't a big deal. But it felt like it. My chest hadn't stopped hurting since I'd given it back to him. But Mase never mentioned it again or acted upset.

He'd held my hand, and we'd walked down the beach. He had persuaded me to eat a few more bites of the cake, and then we had cuddled in the chaise longue and watched the moonlight on the water.

The only thing that had been wrong was **that he** didn't kiss me again. He didn't look at me with those hooded eyes full of need. It was as if he was holding me at arm's length while he was right there with me. Before, he had been flirty and playful.

After the key, that all changed. He changed.

Once we got back to the apartment, he told me to go ahead and use the bathroom first. He'd get ready for bed after me. He hadn't been overcome with desire for me or pulled me into his arms once we were in the privacy of my apartment. He had been kind and polite, but that was it. Nothing more.

I slipped on one of the new pajama sets he'd given me. This one was white with silver piping. I also thought it was the sexiest. Right now, I wanted to see the spark there and know that I hadn't lost him when I didn't take his key.

Why hadn't I? Taking it didn't mean I was using it. He hadn't given it to me thinking I was going to move in the minute I accepted it. He'd said as much. It had been his way of letting me know the offer was there to be accepted when I was ready.

I needed to talk to him.

I had handled this wrong.

I opened the bathroom door and walked to the bedroom.

"No, Cordelia. I'm not there. I'm out of town. I'll be back Sunday, probably. Maybe sooner. Not sure."

I hovered outside the door. Who was Cordelia? My stomach twisted, and my heart sank at hearing him say he might be home sooner. I had really messed up.

"Not my fault if you left them. And no, you can't get into my house with me gone. I left it locked up . . . Cord, come on. Stop playing this game with me. Don't be this way."

He was annoyed. And he called her Cord.

"Like I said, I'll be home Sunday," he snapped, then stuck his phone into his pocket with a sigh.

I stepped back from the door and took several calming breaths. That meant nothing. Cordelia could be someone he worked with or was related to. Or she could just be a friend.

"Who was that?" I asked, as I pushed the door open wide. I hadn't meant to ask, but I needed to know.

Mase turned his attention from the floor to me. His gaze slowly ate me up as he took in my new pajamas. When he had finally made it all the way up to my face, his eyes were lit with the heat I'd missed earlier. "I really like French silk," he said, walking over to me.

I almost wept with relief.

His hand settled on my hip and then slid around to cup

my bottom. "You don't like sleeping in panties, do you, baby?"

"No." I watched him as his eyes grew dark and hot.

"Silk covering this ass is more than any man can handle. I want to kiss my freckle. And see it peeking out from under the lace." He turned me around. "Put your hands on the back of the sofa and stick this sweet bottom out for me just a little. Please, Reese." He whispered my name so close to my ear that his breath tickled my skin.

I did exactly as I was told, and his pleased growl made it worth it.

His hands slid down my hips and thighs as he dropped to his knees behind me. Soft lips and the rough stubble on his jaw brushed the backs of my thighs. He kissed a trail up each one until he found the one freckle that I'd never seen but he seemed to love.

The pleased sound in his throat as he kissed that one spot made my knees weak. I held on to the sofa just as his tongue lapped at the spot below my bottom.

"Oh, God." I leaned over to brace myself better, or I was going to end up on the floor.

"I can smell you. I want to spread these legs and kiss you there. Just me, Reese. This is me and you, baby." His voice was strained, and I knew he was giving me the choice. It was why I trusted him so much. He always took special care not to step too far or make me do anything I wasn't ready for.

"OK" was the only word I could form at the moment.

I was expecting him to spread my legs open where I stood, but Mase stood up and scooped me into his arms. My surprised gasp made him smile as he walked me into the bedroom. "My girl belongs on a bed," he said softly, and he placed me gently down on my unmade bed. "Keep looking at me. The whole time, I want those eyes here," he instructed me, as he pointed to his eyes.

I nodded.

He caressed the inside of my calves with extra care. I was having a hard time inhaling air, and he was playing with my legs. What was going to happen when he actually moved his head between my legs?

I had gotten off listening to him on the phone telling me he wanted to do this. But the reality of it was terrifying. I grabbed fistfuls of the covers and watched as Mase's hand moved past my knees, coaxing my legs open by giving my thighs extra-special attention.

"Eyes on mine, Reese." His tone was husky and deep. This was exciting him.

I snapped my gaze back to his, and he winked at me. "That's better. I want those pretty blue eyes on mine. When I kiss you, don't close them. Keep them on me. OK?"

"Yes," I panted out.

The corners of his lips lifted as he lowered his head, keeping his gaze locked on mine. "Open wider for me," he whispered, as he pressed a kiss to my knee.

Wider. Oh, God.

I started to close my eyes, and a little nip of his teeth inside my thigh had my eyes flying back open.

He was grinning at me. "Eyes on me," he repeated. "You close them again, and I'm rolling you over and biting your ass. Something I really fucking want to do. So don't tempt me."

So he was going to *bite* me if I closed my eyes? Oh, God.

Mase trailed kisses down the insides of my thighs. His eye-lids lowered until he had that sexy hooded look that made me shiver. I was making little noises I didn't even recognize. But seeing Mase's head moving downward was causing a riot of sensations in my body.

He growled as his mouth reached its destination, and his eyes sparked with a hungry look just before I felt his tongue graze over where it throbbed the most.

When he closed his lips around that small spot and sucked, I bucked my hips, unable to stop myself, and cried out his name.

"Eyes, Reese. Give me your eyes now, baby."

"I can't . . . don't stop," I begged.

His tongue slid back over me and then circled my clit. "I don't want to stop. I'll do this for fucking ever if you want, but I need you to look at me. Watch me. See who's making you feel good. Stay here with me."

I forced my eyes open, and his gaze immediately locked with mine. I loved his eyes.

"There's those pretty eyes I dream about," he murmured, as he continued using his tongue to give me a form of pleasure I had never imagined existed.

With each stroke of his tongue, I felt the pressure building inside. The explosion was coming. My legs were shaking, and my vision was starting to blur. Mase's name was falling from my lips over and over, but I couldn't make myself stop.

"That's it," he encouraged. His sexy whisper only made it worse, as the warmth of his breath tickled where his tongue had been. "Give it to me. Let me have it. Ride it out on my face."

With those final words, I came apart.

Mase

I was certain nothing would ever be that beautiful in my lifetime.

Lifting my head, I pressed a kiss to the inside of her thigh. Before she could completely come back from her high, I moved to lie beside her so I could pull her into my arms and hold her. She'd never left me one time. Her eyes had been full of desire. Not once had I seen the fear there, and I had been watching closely. When I had asked her to let me go down on her, I knew I was asking for a lot. I was prepared to stop the moment she panicked.

But she'd stayed with me. No darkness from her past came to take that away from us. When she'd cried out my name and shuddered underneath me, in that moment, I'd felt like the king of the world.

Her eyes fluttered against her cheek as she opened them back up. I hadn't insisted that she keep them open when the orgasm hit her. She'd been lost in her own pleasure then, and I'd wanted her there. I'd enjoyed the way it coursed through her body and took her away for a moment.

Holding her tightly to me, I pressed a kiss to each of her eyelids. She made a soft little sound that reminded me of a kitten. It was almost a purr.

"What have you done to me, Reese Ellis?"

She tilted her head back and looked up at me. "I think that was *you* doing something to *me*," she replied, with a shy but satisfied smile on her lips.

Chuckling, I buried my face in her hair and inhaled. "God, baby, you have no idea. You've got me so fucking wrapped up. And I don't even care."

Reese turned toward me and ran her hand over my head, slipping her fingers into the leather string I used to pull it back. With a tug, she freed my hair, then wrapped my locks around her fingers as she played with it, still smiling like she owned the secret to all happiness.

"I love your hair," she whispered.

"Next time I kiss your sweet pussy, I want your hands in my hair," I told her, closing my eyes as she began to massage my scalp.

"I'm afraid I'd forget myself and pull it."

"It would be so fucking hot if you did."

A soft giggle from her made me smile.

We cuddled in silence for several minutes. Her hands stayed in my hair, playing with it and rubbing my head. I had never been so content.

"Thank you for tonight. I've only had a birthday cake and a party once in my life that I can remember. And it ended up being a day I'd rather forget. But you just gave me a fairy-tale birthday party. I feel special."

Her admission sent that painful slice through me. *Shit.* I hated hearing how this beautiful woman had been so fucking abused and neglected. She deserved a fairy-tale life, but she had lived through hell instead. I was going to spend the rest of our lives making sure she had birthday parties that were fit for a fucking queen. When we were old and gray, she'd have so many good memories that she wouldn't remember the bad ones. I was going to spend my life erasing that shit.

"My best present was you," she said, and pressed a kiss to my jaw.

All my anger at the injustice of her life faded away. She was safe and in my arms. She was mine.

Reese

The ringing of a phone woke me up. Sitting up, I looked around and squinted against the sunlight coming in through the window. The ringing stopped, and I heard the shower running in the bathroom. Mase had left the door wide open. Was that an invitation to peek? Because I really wanted to see him naked and wet.

Grinning, I had thrown back the covers and started to get up when the phone dinged and vibrated on the bed. Looking around, I saw Mase's slim silver phone lying just below his pillow. I grabbed it. I could use that as my excuse for coming into the bathroom while he was showering. Not that he'd expect an excuse.

Knowing Mase, he was hoping I would.

I covered my mouth to suppress a giggle, and his phone dinged and vibrated again. Someone was really trying to get in touch with him. I stopped grinning, and the idea that it could be an emergency hit me.

I glanced down at the phone to see a text message from someone named Major. I didn't mean to read it, but my eyes focused on the words *her panties*, and I couldn't stop myself.

Sliding my finger over the screen, I opened the text message.

> Major: Cord came by insisting she left her panties under
> your bed from the other night. She was determined to get
> them. I let her in. But dude, she seemed pissed at you. You
> done fucking her?

I reread that text over and over. It wasn't my text to read. I was invading Mase's privacy, but I couldn't stop. *Cord. Cordelia.* He had been on the phone with her before. He was . . . he was *fucking* her?

Her panties . . .

The other night . . .

Oh, God. I was going to be sick.

The urge to throw his phone against the wall and scream until all the pain in my chest melted away was strong. How could he do this? My Mase was so good to me. He was sweet and thoughtful. He was patient with me, and he took care of me.

And he was . . . a liar.

I had trusted him.

Everything in my body went numb. Except for my heart, which had ruptured in my chest.

The shower shut off, and I finally moved from the spot I had been frozen in. I swiped my finger over the text message and paused only a brief second to think it through before pressing delete. Then I put his phone back where he had left it. Without looking toward the bathroom, I walked out of the bedroom and as far across the apartment as I could. I stood in the corner farthest from him and waited.

He would come looking for me. I didn't want him getting close.

I couldn't let myself think about all the places he had touched me. When he was gone, he was touching her. She was having sex with him.

It all made sense now. How he was so patient with me. He didn't need sex from me. He was getting it regularly back in Texas. I placed a hand over my mouth to keep from screaming in agony.

This was too much. I hadn't known it could feel like this. The sudden, brutal end of love.

I had never loved before, but now that it was over, the pain was excruciating.

I wouldn't do this again. Love. The happiness it gave you was a fleeting thing. It wasn't worth this.

His body filled the doorway. A towel was wrapped around his hips, and his hair was still dripping water that trailed down his bare chest. "Reese?" his voice was concerned.

He was concerned about me a lot. The broken girl who needed help. I couldn't read, write, or have sex. He was going to fix me. Was that what I had been to him? A project?

"What's wrong, baby?" he asked, as he began to walk toward me. I couldn't let him touch me. Not anymore.

"No!" I screamed, holding my hands up to keep him back. "Don't come near me," I warned.

He stopped, but the look in his eyes was one that I would have once thought was fear. I didn't think that anymore. He didn't know what fear was. Or pain.

"Reese, what's wrong?" he asked carefully, studying me.

"Leave. I want you to leave. Don't come back. I don't want you here." I held my hands up, but I turned my gaze to the door. I couldn't look at him, because my heart was confused. It thought it saw pain in his eyes. It didn't. I had thought I'd seen a lot of things when he looked at me that I didn't truly see.

"Baby, what happened? Don't do this. Don't push me away. Let me come to you."

He thought this was because of my past. I could hear it in his voice. He was talking to the broken girl. The one he felt sorry for. The one he pitied. "I want you gone. Get dressed and get out!" I yelled the last part. He wasn't listening to me. I wanted him to leave. I couldn't stand here like this much longer. The shattering inside my chest made me want to curl up and hold myself together.

"I'm not leaving you, Reese. You have to tell me what's wrong. I can help you—"

"No! I'm not your personal charity case. I was fine before you, and I'll be fine after you. But you need to leave! I'm calling the cops if you aren't out of here in five minutes."

Mase started coming toward me again, and I screamed at the top of my lungs. "Jesus, Reese! What's wrong?" He was yelling now, too.

I leveled my gaze on him. "You. You are wrong. You're wrong for me. I don't want you here. I want you to leave me alone. You've forced me to do things I didn't want to do. You've touched me in places I don't like to be touched. I don't want to see you again. Ever. Just go!"

Saying those words hurt. They were a lie. He would know they were a lie, but I was desperate. He wasn't leaving. He wasn't listening.

When I saw him turn and walk back away, I almost collapsed. He was going to leave me.

The realization that Mase was going to walk out that

door and not come back destroyed whatever part of me was left.

I should never have loved. I wasn't meant to love or be loved. This was a lesson I should have learned by now.

I wanted the numbness to spread, but it was fading. Loss engulfed me.

If only I'd never known how it felt to believe I was special to someone else.

Mase reappeared, and he was holding his duffel in his hand. He walked toward the door without looking at me but stopped just before he got there. His eyes closed tightly, and he let out an unsteady breath. "I'm sorry," was all he said.

Then he walked to the door and opened it. With one more long pause, he stood there. I waited for him to walk away and leave me here alone. Again.

"When you realize what you've said and what you've done, call me. I'll be waiting. I want to hold you more than anything right now and help you get through this, but you won't let me near you. So I'm going to do what you want, because I can't fix everything for you. This time, you have to do it yourself. But when it sinks in that you were wrong, call me, Reese. I'll be waiting. I'll wait forever if I have to."

Then Mase Manning walked out of my door and out of my life.

Mase

When the door had closed behind me, I dropped my bag and bent over, bracing my hands on my knees to suck in air. Reminding myself that she had to work through this was hard. Leaving her . . . Oh, God, I couldn't just fucking leave her. She was in a goddamn corner looking completely destroyed, and I didn't know why.

Each breath hurt. The tightness in my chest was like a vise grip on my lungs. My heart was in that apartment. Walking away without it seemed impossible. But if I was going to get a chance at a future with Reese, she had to let me in. The past haunted her. It was controlling her. That motherfucking low-life scum had done this to her. I'd thought I could hold her through it all and give her so much love she'd overcome it. But those demons were there in her eyes.

All I was doing was helping her pretend they weren't there. I wasn't helping her destroy them and overcome them. My love wasn't enough. I wanted it to be. God, I wanted it to be enough. But she needed to find the strength inside herself.

When she did, she could accept that I loved her. That I adored her. That I wanted her and all the shit in her past. I wanted everything.

Standing up, I winced at the pain.

I didn't walk to my truck. Instead, I went to Jimmy's apartment. I couldn't leave her without knowing someone was watching over her. When she needed me to rescue her, someone had to call me. I knew she never would.

She might not want me, but I'd be damned if I'd let her need me.

Knocking on Jimmy's door, I tried to take a deep breath. But I couldn't.

The door swung open, and his smile immediately turned into a frown. "Mase?"

He had been expecting someone else. I didn't really want to think about that, considering he was wearing a pair of red silk pajama pants and his chest was bare and oiled.

"She wants me to leave. No, she ordered me to leave," I corrected myself. "But I need you to call me if she needs anything. Don't let her suffer. She may think she doesn't want me, but I'll drop anything to get to her."

Jimmy sagged against the door. He looked let-down. "Well, shit. What is in that girl's head? She's crazy about you."

It was her past. Those fucking demons in her memory. But I couldn't tell him that.

"She needs me, you call me. I'll be here."

He nodded.

I gripped the handle of my bag and fought back the emotion. This was it. I was really leaving her. "Watch over her. Make sure she's safe and locked in at night. Don't let her walk to work. Don't let her walk home, either. Keep her safe for me. Please." I was begging him. But at this point, I'd beg anyone.

Tears filled his eyes. "Shit. That girl," he shook his head.

"She's got something in her past she's hiding, but it's dark. I've seen it in her eyes. She'll call you. She loves you."

I hoped to God he was right. "When I'm gone, she'll need someone. Be that someone."

He wiped at his tears, then nodded. "I will."

"Thanks."

I headed back to the stairs and my truck.

I tossed my bag onto the backseat but paused before I got inside. I couldn't leave without telling her.

I stalked back to her door with a purpose and knocked. She didn't come, but I waited.

"Reese. I know you hear me," I said through the door.

I knocked again, but she didn't answer.

"I'm leaving. You want me to go, so I'll go. But know that I love you. I will love you the rest of my life. If you don't call me, I will still be there in Texas loving you."

I waited, but she never came to the door.

After several minutes, I knew she wasn't coming. She was going to let me do this.

Unable to stop myself, I banged on the door with my fist one more time and yelled as loudly as I could, "I love you, Reese Ellis! I love you so fucking much!"

I heard a door open next door, but I didn't look at whoever it was. I waited outside her door, hoping she'd open it.

But she didn't.

Reese

Nine weeks later

I opened my door to find Jimmy on the other side. He had a cappuccino in each hand. Once that was a comforting sight. Nothing comforted me anymore. The nightmares from my past were back with a vengeance. I rarely slept anymore. Cappuccino in the morning and coffee in a mug in the afternoon were the only way I made it through work every day.

"Ready, sunshine?" he asked.

I nodded and grabbed my backpack. "Yeah," I replied, taking the cup he offered me.

"I hate you. I want your skin. It's not fair you get so tanned," he complained.

"I work out in the sun. Of course I'm going to get tanned," I reminded him, rolling my eyes. He whined about my tan at least twice a week.

"Tanning and watching hot men swing clubs. I'm working in the wrong department," he said with a huff.

We both knew that Darla wouldn't let him work on the golf course at the Kerrington Club. Jimmy had a face women loved. He worked as a server, and the women came in droves to flirt with him and tip him well. On the course, he wouldn't be as popular. There were several women who golfed but not many. The majority played tennis. The men dominated the golf course.

"It's hot out there, and the men are all dressed in shorts and polo shirts. It's not exactly sexy attire. You aren't missing out on anything."

Jimmy opened his car door and rolled his eyes at me. "Girl, I've seen Rush Finlay's hot ass in shorts and a polo, and it's enough for me to pour ice water down my pants."

"God! Jimmy!" I couldn't help but laugh, but honestly, he could be so descriptive.

I sank down into the passenger seat, put my backpack on the floor, and set my coffee in the cupholder so I could buckle up. Riding with Jimmy to and from work was easier now that we worked at the same place. Jimmy had arranged it so that our schedules matched every week.

"Keeping it real, babe," he replied, as he climbed inside.

Sometimes Jimmy keeping it real was him just wanting to make me laugh. Only recently had he been able to accomplish that, and it wasn't often. But I would give him one thing: since the moment Mase Manning had walked out of my life, Jimmy had been my shadow.

I couldn't go anywhere without checking in with him. He panicked if he didn't know where I was, and he always stayed late with me. For a while, he would sit and hold my hand while I went to sleep at night. He never mentioned it, but I knew he was trying to take the place of my nightly phone calls. The ones I didn't have anymore.

I had quit my cleaning job with the Carters simply because I couldn't see anyone who reminded me of Mase, and there was the chance that he'd turn up anytime for a visit. I wasn't sure how I'd handle that. I also told Blaire Finlay that I couldn't clean for her. The Finlays also reminded me of Mase.

Once I was jobless, Jimmy offered to get me work as a cart girl on the country club's golf course. I had told him about my dyslexia then, and he had helped me fill out the application. When he had asked me if I wanted to read to him at night, I had broken down and closed myself up in my room. He didn't have to ask to figure out why. He was a smart guy.

Now he asked me, "Thad still coming a lot during your shifts?"

I sighed and laid my head back against the seat. "Thad just golfs a lot. He's not only coming during my shifts."

Jimmy let out an amused laugh. "Keep telling yourself that, chick. But blondie doesn't golf unless he's with Woods or Grant. It isn't something I ever saw him do by himself. Until you put on that little outfit and started passing out beers."

I didn't want to think about Thad coming to see me. I didn't want anyone coming to see me. Not that way.

I love you, Reese Ellis!

That broken cry that had been so loud my neighbors heard it was all that took up residence in my chest. Everything else was gone. Finding any emotion was hard for me. Only at night, when I was asleep and the past came back to torture me, did I scream and cry.

Over the past nine weeks, I had dealt with moments of weakness. Once I almost convinced myself that I had imagined that text message. And when I couldn't make myself believe that, I tried to convince myself that I could live with him having sex with other people. If I had him in my life, that would be enough. I would forgive him for needing sex so badly that he had to get it elsewhere.

Then, at my lowest points, I blamed myself for being screwed-up in the head. For not being able to give him what his body needed. I had pushed him into her arms.

He loved me, though. He had yelled it at the top of his lungs.

After weeks of no word from him, I had to accept that he had moved on. I had sent him away, and he had gone. Not easily, but he had gone. Now someone else, probably Cordelia, was taking care of his needs. She was loving him and making him smile. She was everything I hadn't been to him.

So I just survived. Every day, I got up and survived the day. Every night, I survived the nightmares. Then I did it again. Over and over.

And alone.

Because I'd made him leave.

"Earth to Reesey-poo. Where did you go, woman? I asked you a question."

I shook my Mase thoughts away. They'd be back to fill the void later. "Sorry, what did you ask?"

"I asked if you wanted to go take your written test and get your driving permit tomorrow since we're off work."

Dr. Munroe had been helping me study for two weeks now. I was as prepared as I'd ever be. "Yeah. That would be good," I replied.

The excitement didn't come. I had thought once that I would never drive a car. Now I was close to achieving that goal, and I couldn't manage to feel even a little joy. Because the one person I wanted with me, the one person I wanted to share this with, wasn't here.

I had pushed him away. I had loved too much. With a broken mind and body, I had loved completely. And he had needed more than that broken mind and body.

Images of him touching a faceless woman and doing things to her that he did to me shredded me every time I let myself think about it. I wanted to be whole. I wanted to be enough for him.

"Don't get too excited. I might have to pull over until you calm down," Jimmy said sarcastically.

I forced a smile for him.

"Not buying that fake shit, Reese," he replied.

It was all I had. Fake shit.

Mase

Swinging the ax, I split the piece of wood I needed to mend the fence. But I couldn't stop. Lifting the ax, I swung again, ruining the perfect piece I'd created. Then I swung again. And again. And again.

I wasn't sure when the yelling started, but when I looked up to see my mother standing across from me with her hands on her hips, frowning at me disapprovingly, I knew I must have gotten loud.

Shit.

She had been waiting for me to snap. I had been careful to work through my day without emotion as long as her attention was on me. Getting Maryann Colt off your back when she thought you needed to talk was near impossible.

I dropped the ax and stared down at the small chunks of wood that were now only good for firewood. I'd annihilated it. I would have to go get another piece now so I could fix the goddamn fence.

"Don't reckon that wood did anything to you," Momma said, cocking one of her eyebrows.

I didn't respond. I just dropped to my haunches and started picking up the mess I'd made.

"I've had all I can take, Mase Colt Manning. You've been a shell of my boy for months, and now you lose your mind and begin yelling and beating the shit outta that log with an ax? You have to talk to me. You're giving me anxiety attacks. I'm worried about you."

For nine weeks, I had managed to live without my heart. This wasn't a life. My life was a woman who didn't want me. This was an existence. An empty, shallow existence.

I hadn't told my mother about Reese, but Harlow had. Momma had asked me about her the week after Reese sent me away from her. I had been so overcome with pain from just the sound of her name that I had jumped up and fled the table. Momma hadn't mentioned her again.

But now I needed her to. I needed to talk about Reese. I wanted to tell someone about her. To fill my emptiness with the memory of her.

"I love her," I said simply.

She raised both of her eyebrows now. "I kind of got that already, sweetie. When you ran like the fires of hell were after you the day I asked you about her, you gave that away."

"She's my life, Momma. Reese. She's it. My one. But she doesn't want me." Just saying it sent a bolt of agony through me. I winced, unable to hide it from my mother.

"Then she's a fool," Momma said, with all the conviction of a mother who loved her son.

"No. She's brilliant. She's beautiful. She's like a bright ray of sunlight. She's . . . Her life growing up . . ." I stopped and swallowed the bile that rose in my throat just from thinking about what she'd been through. How my girl had suffered. "It was bad, Momma. Dark. As dark and twisted as a girl's life can be. But she's not a fool."

My mother's face fell. I could see her fighting back the tears in her eyes. "Oh, baby. I should have figured when my big-hearted, beautiful boy fell in love, he'd fall in love so completely. You never did anything halfway. You didn't take your first steps, you took off running. You didn't say your first word, you sang an entire line of a song. And you didn't just take up for the underdogs at school, you got expelled for tying a bully to a flagpole. My baby has never done anything halfway. You do it with so much determination it blasts everyone else's attempts out of the water."

She walked around my mess and dropped down beside me. I felt the tears burn my eyes as she took my face in her hands and looked at me with so much love and heartache, because that was who she was. My mom hurt with me. She always had.

"You are a good man. The best. I love your stepfather, but even his doesn't compare to the heart you have. You were the best thing I'll ever do in this life. I can't top creating you. Being your mother is a gift that brings me joy every day of my life. I'll die knowing I left a man on this earth who will leave a trail of good everywhere he goes." She stopped, and I knew there was a "but" coming. "But for the first time in your life, I am watching you let someone destroy you. I miss your smile and your laugh. I want those back. You've never let any obstacle in your life go unconquered. Why are you doing it now? If you love her, then go get her. No woman in her right mind can turn this face down."

I reached over and wiped the tears from my mother's determined face. "I need her to come to me. If we have a chance at a future, I need her to come to me. I've always taken what I wanted and conquered my trials, but nothing and no one has ever meant what she does. I can't conquer her, Momma. I love her. I never want to make her do anything. Even love me. She has to love me all on her own."

Momma let out a sob and wrapped her arms around me and held me to her. I closed my eyes and fought back the emotion threatening to let go. The last time my mother had seen me cry was when I was three and broke my arm falling off a trampoline. Even when Harlow had lain in a coma, I had cried in private.

I would never get over losing Reese. If she never came back to me, I'd be broken the rest of my life.

Reese

Another week passed by, and I managed to survive. It was all I was doing. With every day that went by, I felt like I was losing myself a little more. The horror of my past was slowly taking over. The progress I had achieved over the two years I'd been away was gone. I could no longer push away the memories of my stepfather.

Soon I would have to see a therapist. I wasn't sleeping much at all now, and when I did, it wasn't peaceful. The weight was falling off me, and I had dark circles under my eyes that I couldn't cover up anymore. I needed help.

The only thing holding me back was that I knew I'd have to talk about Mase.

I couldn't talk about him. It hurt too much.

"Reese Ellis?" a female voice asked. I put down the beers I was loading into the drink cart's icebox and turned around.

An attractive older lady with dark hair that curled under in a shoulder-length bob stood looking at me as if she was studying me. I knew she wasn't a member here. The worn-out jeans and boots she was wearing didn't look like anything the ladies here wore. Then there was the cowboy hat that sat back on her head. That was a dead giveaway that she was out of place.

"Yes?" I replied.

She didn't smile or say anything right away. She continued to take me in. Although she wasn't glaring at me, she looked as if she wanted to shake me.

I glanced around to see if there was anyone else around or just us.

"I imagined you'd be beautiful, but just like always, when my boy does something, he does it big," she said, and a sad smile touched her lips.

I didn't know what she was talking about or who she thought she was talking to. Saying thank you didn't seem like the right thing to do.

"Those dark circles and the empty look in your eyes tell me all I need to know. So let me tell you what *you* need to know," she said, taking a few steps toward me. "I've watched my son fight battles for everyone he's ever loved and win. When he was seven, his cousin got picked on at school by a bully. My baby found out. The next thing I know, I have to go get my boy from school because he was suspended for wrapping another kid around the flagpole with duct tape. I was horrified. Until I found out the kid was the one who had been beating on his cousin. Calling him names and knocking him down in the halls. That particular day, the bully had stuck his cousin's head in the toilet, with urine in it, and flushed. After the duct tape, no one messed with his cousin again.

"When he was ten, the librarian at his school, who brought him cookies every day and always saved him the best books, was being let go because the school board said they didn't have the budget to keep a full-time librarian. Mrs. Hawks was in her seventies, but she loved those kids, and my boy was her favorite. So my baby got a petition together and then got different businesses in town to pledge funds and donate to the cause. Mrs. Hawks didn't lose her job. In fact, he collected so much money she got a raise.

"When he was nineteen, he found out his little sister had gotten her heart broken at school by a boy who only cared about who her daddy was. He asked me if he could go visit her, and I let him go. That boy who broke his little sister's heart found his truck just out of town, completely immersed in water."

She stopped and chuckled. "Mase Colt Manning fights for those he loves. It's what he does. And I know he tried to fight for you. He wanted to conquer your battles. And from the little research I've done, I found out he sends a monthly check to a Dr. Astor Munroe that costs more than I care to share. He gets weekly reports from this professor on a Reese Ellis's progress. He's fighting your battles. Which means he loves you, too. Problem is, my baby goes big when he does anything. And when he decided to fall in love, he did it in a massive way."

She stopped and pointed her finger at me. I could see her son now in the determined gaze she leveled on me. How had I not seen it before?

"He needs someone to fight for him now. Because he's lost himself. He's a shell of the man I raised. He's walking through life with no joy, because he tells me he left it with his heart. He left it with you. So if you love him even a tiny smidgen as much as he loves you, then fight for him. He deserves it more than anyone. It's time someone fought his battle."

A drop fell on my arm, and I reached up to feel my face wet with tears. My heart was back, and it was twisting in pain listening to Mase's mother tell me how he needed me. He was hurt because of me.

I didn't care anymore about the text. Or the other woman. If Mase needed me to fight for him, I would. I'd fight whoever the hell Cordelia was, too. I would fight until I couldn't fight anymore.

"Where is he?" I asked.

"He's at home. He thinks I've gone to visit my sister in San Antonio."

"How do I get to him? Where is his home?"

A smile spread across the other woman's face. "I can take you right to him."

I closed the lid on the cooler. "Let me go tell my boss I'm leaving. Then I'll be ready to go."

"I'm Maryann Colt, by the way," she said, holding out her hand for me to shake. "And it is a pleasure to meet the woman my son loves. I was worried, but I can see he chose well."

Her approval sent the first warmth through me that I'd felt in ten weeks, two days, and five hours.

Mase

"OK, I'm a douchebag. I have to 'fess up, because this shit is eating me alive," Major said, as he stepped into the barn with a saddle thrown over his shoulder.

I continued rubbing down my Appaloosa, Kryptonite, and ignored his comment. I had to get the stallion's stall cleaned out next, and I didn't have time to deal with Major and his drama.

"I'm fucking Cordelia. I've been fucking her for like two months. She's really good at sucking my dick. Sorry, but I'm a man, and she came on to me, and I let her blow me. Then I turned her over the sawhorse and fucked her. It was a weak moment. I was horny, and she came strutting in wearing these cutoff jeans shorts that showed part of her ass and a little top that barely covered her tits. She's hot, man. I asked you if you were still fucking her, and you didn't answer. I figured it meant she didn't matter."

That was why Cordelia had left me the hell alone. I should be giving Major money for this. "Glad she's servicing you well." I patted Kryptonite, then turned to lead him over to the stall I'd already cleaned.

"So you don't care that I'm tapping that ass?" he asked.

"You did me a favor. She wasn't taking no for an answer."

Major let out a sigh of relief. "Thank God. I was worried you've been in this sour mood because I took your go-to fuck."

I didn't even respond to that. There was no point.

"The day she came to get her panties, I was close to fucking her then. She was dressed in a little short skirt, looking like a damn porn star. But I called and texted you, and you didn't answer. I let her go then. But the next day, when she showed up in the barn, I fucked her. You weren't coming out of your house that week. It was that week you were in such a bad mood."

Right on time. He started things up with her when I really needed everyone out of my face. No telling what I would have said to her if she'd started that shit up then. I didn't want her, but I didn't see any use in saying anything hurtful. She didn't deserve that.

"Where were you that weekend, anyway? That time I texted you? You came back here angry at the world. And you've been fucked-up ever since. Was it Rosemary Beach? That girl you were going to see?"

I wasn't talking about this with him.

Wait. What text?

The world around me stopped, and my empty chest suddenly felt heavier than lead. *Please, God, no. Don't let this be what I think it is.*

"Major," I said, almost afraid to ask. Did I want the answer? Could I live with this?

"Yeah?"

"What text?" I asked, before I could stop myself.

"The one I sent you about Cord getting her panties under your bed and asking if you were still fucking her."

No . . . no . . . no . . .

"Major, I never got that text. When did you send it?"

"I told you—"

"No. I need to know the date and time you sent that motherfucking text!" I shouted. The horses whinnied, but my head was pounding, and the heaviness was taking over my lungs.

"Shit, dude. I'll check. Calm down," he grumbled, pulling out his phone and scrolling through the text messages.

"Uh . . . June 29 at nine a.m. Called twice before that, too. No answer or response."

I dropped the supplies from my hands and walked out the door. I kept walking. I just fucking walked. I walked until I was as far away from Major as I could get, until my house vanished from sight.

Then I tilted my head back and let it all out in an angry roar.

She'd seen that text. That was what had sent her to the corner, looking at me as if she had shattered. A fucking text had taken her from me.

Reese

Maryann Colt had talked the whole way on the drive from the airport. She had slept for the entire flight. I hadn't been able to do anything but stare out the window. My thoughts had been on Mase and the boy she'd described. He sounded exactly like the man I had fallen in love with. One text had made me doubt everything. All he had done to show me how much he loved me, and I hadn't even let him explain.

I hadn't been a charity case. He wasn't trying to fix me. He was fighting my battles because he loved me.

He didn't even know about the text. I had deleted it before putting his phone back. He had no idea what had changed that morning. I was now going to show up at his house unannounced. I knew that just because his mother said he wanted me, that didn't mean I wouldn't have to fight for him.

He could have moved on in other ways. Cordelia could be keeping him warm at night. I wouldn't think about that.

I listened to Maryann talk instead. I had to focus on her words, not on what I could be facing soon. But no matter what it was, I would fight. He had fought for me once. I was going to fight for him now.

"His house is up the road a bit. He might be in bed by now.

It's late, and he's been going straight to sleep after dinner. But knock on the window to the left side of the house if he doesn't open the door. I'm gonna let you walk from here. I don't want him to see my truck. It's all on you now. You go show my boy he's worth fighting for."

I opened the truck door and jumped down.

Maryann pointed to the dirt road lit by moonlight right behind her house. "Follow that trail. It'll take you right to his door."

I started to walk that way, then stopped and glanced back at her. I caught her wiping her eyes. "Thank you," I said. "I know you did it for him. But you saved me, too."

I didn't wait for her response. I headed up the hill toward the rooftop I could barely see in the distance. The metal roof caught the moon's rays, and I followed them. My heart was racing for the first time in months. I was going to see him. I was going to see Mase.

If Cordelia was there, I had to keep my calm and not claw her eyes out. But the closer I got to his cabin, the more I realized I couldn't *not* attack her if she was touching him. If he had touched her.

I was going to make myself sick. I couldn't think about that.

There was a black truck similar to the silver one his mother drove parked outside. It was the only vehicle, and I wanted to sigh in relief. I could fight the Cordelia battle later. Right now, I was going to focus on getting him to forgive me.

I stepped up onto the front porch and stopped. Now that I was here without Maryann coaching me, I was frozen in fear. But I had come this far. Flown for the first time in my life and left the only safe place I'd ever known to come here. To face a man I had thrown out of my life.

The last time I'd heard his voice, he'd been shouting through my door that he loved me.

Did he still? Had I waited too long?

The door swung open before I even got close enough to knock, revealing a shirtless Mase. The shadows covered his face, but I knew that chest. I also knew those boxer briefs. I had to say something. My entire body seemed to freeze up on me.

"I came to fight for you," I blurted out, and then I burst into tears.

Mase

Reese was here. At my house. On my porch. And she was crying.

I stepped out into the darkness, still wondering if this was a dream and if I had somehow managed to get some sleep tonight after all.

"Reese?" I asked, afraid that if I touched her, I'd wake up.

"I'm sorry. I . . . seeing you . . . I was going to be strong and tell you I love you and I messed up and I love you and—"

Fuck the dream. I reached for her and pulled her into my arms.

She was here. She was here. She was here.

Her arms wrapped around me and held on tightly. Just the way I remembered. The sweet cinnamon met my nose, and I knew my imagination wasn't that good. I'd tried to imagine her smell more than once and couldn't. This was my Reese.

"I love you. I won't leave. I'm here to make you take me back. I'm empty without you." She sobbed in my arms.

Was she trying to persuade me to let her stay with me? Did she seriously think she had to beg for me to keep her?

"Reese, I—"

She pulled back and looked up at me with wide, panicked

eyes. "No. Don't say anything. Just listen to me. I was wrong. You're worth fighting for. I was . . . I am a mess. I have to overcome a lot, but I will make it worth it. I will love you more than she ever could. More than anyone ever could. I'll spend the rest of my life proving to you that I'm worth the hassle. I won't let a day go by without showing you how much I love you. I'll move here. I'll get a place and a job. I will cook you meals, and I'll—"

I covered her mouth with mine and stopped her adorable, rambling argument. Her surprised cry was followed by a whimper, and she kissed me like she needed the taste of me to live. Her sweetness seeped into me, as those plump lips pressed against mine. I cupped her face and pulled her back so that I could look into her eyes.

They were still watery from her instant breakdown when she saw me. But they were beautiful. My beautiful baby-blues. The ones that I dreamed about. The ones that would always hold me.

"I'm worth fighting for?" I asked, wanting to hear her say that one more time. She had looked so damn determined when she'd said it the first time.

"Yes!" she said, the fierceness coming back.

"And who do you think you have to fight against for me?"

Pain flickered in her eyes. I didn't want that. I started to assure her that there was no one, but she spoke first. "Anyone . . . I'll fight anyone," she said finally.

She was talking about Cordelia. That motherfucking text.

"Baby. From the moment those lips of yours touched mine, I was yours. No, scratch that. From the moment I walked out of the bedroom and saw your sweet ass in the air and heard you singing off key, I was yours. No one else. Ever. Before you, yes, there were others. And there was one girl I had a 'friends with benefits' relationship with. Nothing else. But the moment you walked into my life, that ended. She didn't take it well, and she tried to get me to change my mind. But all I saw, all my heart saw, was *you*. No one else."

"Cordelia," she said softly.

"Yes. But the text you saw from Major was because I came home from work to find her in my bed. I ordered her out and threatened to call my momma if she didn't get out of my bed. I even washed my sheets to get rid of her smell. Hell, I've even bought a new mattress since then and new sheets. I didn't want to sleep on anything that had anyone but you on it. Ever."

"She left her panties that day," she said softly, her eyes shining with new tears. "That was what the text meant."

I nodded. I tucked a lock of her hair behind her ear. "If I'd known that was what had you looking at me like I was a monster, I would have stayed and fought for you. But I thought it was the past, the demons that haunt you. I thought I had pushed too hard and you needed space." I stopped and took a deep breath. "I thought you would call. I waited. I was waiting. I was going to wait forever."

She puckered up again, and I started kissing her face. I didn't want her to cry. I had her here. With me.

"I'm not letting you go back. You're staying with me. I can't let you leave me. I'll go crazy," I told her, as I kissed her cheeks and nose, then pressed a chaste kiss to her mouth.

"I don't want to leave," she said.

God, I loved her. "Come inside," I said, slipping my hand over hers and leading her into the house. "Lie down with me. I want to hold you."

Reese stopped, and I looked back at her. "No. Tonight *I* want to hold *you*," she said, her face once again determined.

"If that's what you want," I agreed.

I took off her boots and pulled down her jeans. She let me undress her without question. When I unhooked her bra, I didn't touch or look, I just grabbed my discarded T-shirt and slipped it over her head.

She buried her nose in it and inhaled, wrapping her arms tightly around herself. I loved it when she cuddled with my clothing as if it were me.

Then she crawled up onto my new king-size bed and put her back against the headboard and held out her arms to me.

Emotion battling with amusement, I was able to keep the tears burning my eyes from breaking free. I moved over her and laid my head against her chest so I could listen to her heartbeat.

She ran her fingers through my hair as we lay there like that. I wrapped my arms around her waist and basked in her scent. The sound of her heart sped up every time I slid my hand down toward her bottom, then back up again.

"Every step I've taken in life has led me to you," she said in a whisper. "And because I'm here now, I don't regret one thing. For every bad thing that happened, I've been rewarded something even more beautiful than all of the bad in return. You made it worth it. You're my gift in life. I lived through the bad and survived. My reward was that God gave me you."

I no longer cared about holding back tears.

I cried in her arms.

Reese

Today we were both going back to Rosemary Beach to pack up my things. Mase hadn't been OK with me going anywhere without him, so for two days, I wore clothes that belonged to Harlow from when she had stayed at his house a couple of years ago. They were all too short and snug, but I managed to make do.

However, Mase wouldn't let me out of the house dressed in her clothing. He was worried about someone looking at me. Major had seen me the first morning in a pair of Harlow's shorts and a tank top and offered Mase his left nut for me. Mase had punched him in the face. It had been a fiasco.

When Maryann had come up to the house, upset and asking Mase why he had broken Major's nose, he told her, and she'd started laughing. Then she'd turned right around and left.

I woke up to an empty bed that morning, which, after the way Mase had held me in a vise grip the past two nights, surprised me. I got up and walked toward the bathroom to hear the shower running and Mase singing. Unlike my singing, his was beautiful. His voice had a raspy edge to it, but it flowed in a way that gave me goose bumps. I'd never heard him sing before. With a father like Kiro, it only made sense that he had a voice to match his gene pool.

I didn't recognize the lyrics, but they drew me in. I opened the door and stepped into the steam. He didn't notice me, but his head was tilted back under the water, and he was still singing.

I'll take your demons if you'll let me in. Don't hold it back, baby, because all I want to give is more.

His head turned, and his singing stopped when his eyes locked with mine.

It wasn't one of those things I needed to think about and plan. This man loved me, and I knew I'd never love anyone the way I loved him. He was willing to take anything I threw at him, as long as he could hold me in the end.

Grabbing the hem of my shirt, I pulled it up and over my head and tossed it to the floor. Then I quickly slipped off my panties and went to open the shower door. Mase stood frozen as his gaze trailed down my naked body.

Stepping into the hot stream of water, I looked down at his thick, corded thighs and trailed my gaze up to see that he was hard and ready. Feeling brave and safe, I reached for the soap and began lathering my hands as Mase stood still. He didn't move or even flinch. Only his eyes followed my every move. I moved closer and slid both hands over his hard, smooth length.

A low groan came from his chest, and I looked up at him to see his eyelids had lowered to that hooded expression I loved. Sliding my wet, soapy hands over him with long strokes, I watched as his jaw went lax, and he backed up and leaned against the wall. I moved a hand underneath to cup his tight sack and began soaping him there, too.

"Reese," he moaned, reaching for my hand.

"Let me," I begged, pressing my breasts against his chest.

"Ah . . . fuuuck."

I kept my grip firm and slow as the tip of his penis grew red. Clear fluid began to leak out, and I became anxious to hear him come. I quickened my pace, and his breath hitched.

"I'm gonna . . . come. Shit, baby, I'm gonna come," he said, and then a deep cry fell from his lips as his release shot out onto my stomach and over my hands.

"Don't move." He gasped, and I looked up to see his eyes zoom in on my stomach, covered in him. "Oh, goddamn . . . don't move. Just let me look at you. Like that."

Feeling brave, I ran my fingertip through the white stream of come that had landed on me. Then I lifted my gaze to look at him. His eyes had gone hot again. A possessive gleam shone in them.

"Rub it in," he said in a hoarse whisper.

I did as he said. I used both hands and massaged it into my skin until it was gone.

He reached behind himself and took the bar of soap and began to soap his hands. Moving away from the wall, he closed the space between us until his hands covered my breasts. Then he began to wash me. Or them. Thoroughly. He pinched my nipples and squeezed them gently before moving down my stomach. When he got to where I'd rubbed his release into my skin, he washed it with a reverent touch that made the ache between my legs turn into a throb.

By the time he moved his hand between my legs, I had to put both my hands out to hold on to the wall on either side of me. My legs began to buckle, and Mase whispered in my ear that I was beautiful. That I was his. That he loved every part of me. That seeing his come on me made him crazy with need.

Holding on to his shoulders, I felt the buildup coming, and I knew I was about to be hit with an orgasm that would very likely send me to my knees.

Mase slipped an arm around my waist and held me as he pressed on my clit one more time. He held me while the pleasure crashed over me, and my knees finally gave in and buckled.

By the time I was coming back to earth, he had rinsed me and was carrying me out of the shower. He didn't dry me until he set me on the end of his bed. When he had me dry, he did a quick once-over on himself, then moved me back on the bed.

His mouth covered mine as his hard, naked body brushed up against me. I arched my back, trying to feel more of him as he continued to hold himself up and over me. This would be another reason I was thankful for my long legs. I wrapped them around his waist and forced him down on me.

"Yes, oh, God, yes, that feels good," I said against his mouth, as my breasts were finally smashed against his chest and my center was open to him while his thick erection rubbed against it.

Mase tore his mouth from mine and buried it in my neck. He was breathing hard. And I realized his hands were in tight fists by my head.

"Mase?" I asked, running my fingers down his back, enjoying the feel of the muscles flexed under my touch.

"I want . . . I can't . . . God, baby," he groaned, and his fists clenched as if he was fighting something hard.

I felt the swell of his erection jerk against me, and I knew then. He wanted inside me. I'd been so wrapped up in feeling him close that I hadn't once gotten frightened.

The pain from my past. The pain that I once marked any contact with, sexual or otherwise, was no longer in my life. This man was my world. He loved me. He was gentle and careful with me. And I wanted to be as close to him as possible. I wanted to know what it was like to be one with him. This wasn't dirty or wrong. This was beautiful and pure.

Lifting my hips, I moved my hand down and angled him until his tip was right there at my entrance. In one thrust, we would be joined. This was what sex was made for, a magical connection between two people who loved each other so much they became whole in body, if only for a moment. Just like the hearts they'd already joined together.

"Make love to me, Mase. Show me what love is like. *Please.*" I added the last word to remind him of all the times he'd asked me if he could touch me and ended it with "please." I wanted this as much as he had wanted those things.

"You're my life," he whispered in my ear, as he sank inside of me, filling me up.

Tears filled my eyes, and I wrapped my arms around him and held him close. With a gentleness that I'd only known from him, he began to rock into me, while he kissed my face and neck and told me I was beautiful. That we were beautiful.

I had never known anything could feel this complete.

Sliding my legs up and down his back and his perfectly defined bottom, I sank into the luxury of being loved by Mase.

"I love you," he panted in my ear.

"I love you, too," I said on a small cry.

"I want to come inside you. But I won't until you're ready," he said, as he kissed my neck.

I wanted him inside me. But I wasn't on any birth control. I needed that. I had never had a need for it before.

"God, Reese, you're so tight. I swear, I don't want to ever pull out of you," he said on a growl.

Lifting my legs up so his thrust went deeper, I felt him rub something inside me, and I instantly shot off into the brightest explosion I'd ever felt. His name tore from my lips, and I locked my legs around him and held on so I didn't fall away.

His body shook as he shouted my name. As he jerked above me, I peeled open my eyes to see his eyes closed tightly and his head thrown back. Sweat had broken out on his forehead, and a small drop rolled down his face and landed on me.

When he finally opened his eyes, he looked directly at me. "I can't apologize for that, because, God, Reese, I swear, angels just sang, and this house just rocked on its foundation."

Smiling, I ran my hands through his damp hair and pulled his mouth down to mine. "What would you apologize for?" I asked against his lips.

"For coming inside you," he said in a whisper.

He was still inside me. I'd been so lost in the aftermath of heaven that I hadn't realized it.

"Oh," I replied.

"When you locked your legs, I tried to hold off until you finished, but you're so tight. And you're so damn gorgeous when you get off. And you squeezed me like a glove, baby. I was coming before I realized it."

I wasn't ruining this moment because we'd forgotten ourselves. "Mase, that was . . . that was more . . . more than I ever imagined."

He rolled over onto his back, still buried inside of me. I liked that he wasn't in a hurry to leave me. I wanted him as close as possible. I was now on top of him. "I love you. You're my world. But there are two things running a really close second," he said in a serious tone. "Those long legs of yours and that tight little pussy are going to own me if you're not careful," he added with a teasing grin.

Laughing, I kissed him. Because he was mine.

Mase

I had written my address with a Sharpie on each box, now stacked by Reese's front door. She was busy cleaning the now-empty fridge. Jimmy had just left after tearfully hugging her during their good-bye.

He'd done just as I asked. He'd been there for her. He had kept her safe. And I owed the man one. I wasn't sure how I would repay him, but I would. Somehow.

Reese bent over, distracting me as her shorts rode up her legs and flashed my favorite freckle at me. "Freckle, baby. You want to finish that without my mouth on your ass, then don't bend over," I warned her, as I closed the door and stalked around the boxes toward her.

She stood up and swung around to grin at me. "Sorry. I had to clean the bottom of the fridge."

"Don't apologize. I've decided I want to kiss that ass. Bend back over," I said, with a wicked grin.

Reese backed up, putting her hands in front of her to stop me. "No. We will never get out of here if you don't stop it. We've had sex on the sofa, in bed, over the bar, and on the dresser. And it's only been like thirty-six hours since we got here. We will never finish."

I grabbed her hands and tugged her to me, careful not to hurt her. "Baby, whose pussy is this?" I asked, sliding my hand down the front of her shorts.

"Yours," she said on a sigh.

My possessive monster roared to life. "That's right. And I want to play with my pussy. And hear my girl scream my name."

Reese's eyes glazed over, and her breathing hitched. I knew I had her. She was so easy to convince. The first few times, I had been careful and taken our time. Made sure she was with me and that she knew I worshipped her and would never hurt her.

She didn't need that anymore. All I had to do was talk dirty, and she was melting up against me, ready for me to do whatever I wanted. Again, this woman made me feel like the king of the world.

A knock on the door stopped me from pulling her shirt up and sucking on her tits. I fought back, muttering a curse, because it was probably someone else come to tell her goodbye. Reese needed to know she would be missed. That more people here cared about her than just Jimmy. And for that reason alone, I kept from complaining.

"I'll get it. Miss Popular has more guests," I teased her.

Her musical laugh followed me.

I jerked open the door, expecting to see someone I knew, but instead, I was greeted by a tall, distinguished-looking man dressed in what I knew was an Armani custom suit because I had one for special events. His black hair and olive skin made me think he was Italian. There was something about the way his eyes were shaped. They were brown but familiar.

"Does a Reese Ellis reside here?" he asked, his accent not as thick as I was expecting. He kind of reminded me of the Hollywood version of a Mafia lord.

"She did," I replied, not liking that this man knew Reese's name and was looking for her.

"I'm Reese Ellis," she said, coming up behind me.

Shit. I didn't want her coming to the door. Something about this man concerned me.

"Can I help you?" she asked, studying the man curiously.

"Baby, I got this," I whispered, moving her back behind me with one arm and making sure my body covered her.

The corner of the man's mouth lifted as if he was amused. "I'm glad to see Reese has someone to protect her. However, I've waited twenty-three years to meet her." He held out his hand to me. "I'm Benedetto DeCarlo, Reese's father."

Acknowledgments

First of all, I want to thank the Atria team. The brilliant Jhanteigh Kupihea. I couldn't ask for a better editor. She is always positive and working to make my books the best they can be. Thank you, Jhanteigh, for being awesome. Ariele Fredman for being not only brilliant with your ideas but listening to mine. Judith Curr for giving me and my books a chance. And everyone else at Atria who had a hand in getting this book to production. I love you all.

My agent, Jane Dystel. She is always there to help in any situation. I'm thankful that I have her on my side in this new and ever-changing world of publishing. Lauren Abramo, who handles my foreign rights. I couldn't begin to think of conquering that world without her.

The friends who listen to me and understand me the way no one else in my life can: Colleen Hoover and Jamie McGuire. You two have been with me from the beginning. Knowing I can call you both at any time when I need advice or just an ear is priceless.

My beta readers, Natasha Tomic and Autumn Hull. You both are brilliant and know exactly where to point out what is missing. Thank you so much for keeping up with my hectic schedule. Beta reading for someone who is always writing a book isn't an easy job.

Abbi's Army, which is led by Danielle Lagasse and Natasha Tomic. These two ladies lead a group of readers who support everything I do. They make each release day a success, and when I need a pick-me-up, I can always go to their group and find reasons to smile. They remind me daily why I write books. I love all their faces.

Last but certainly not least:

My family. Without their support I wouldn't be here. My husband, Keith, makes sure I have my coffee and that the kids are all taken care of when I need to lock myself away and meet a deadline. My three kids are so understanding, although once I walk out of that writing cave they expect my full attention, and they get it. My parents, who have supported me all along. Even when I decided to write steamier stuff. My friends, who don't hate me because I can't spend time with them for weeks at a time because my writing is taking over. They are my ultimate support group, and I love them dearly.

My readers. I never expected to have so many of you. Thank you for reading my books. For loving them and telling others about them. Without you I wouldn't be here. It's that simple.